DOWN AND OUT ON MURDER MILE

ALSO BY TONY O'NEILL

Digging the Vein

Seizure Wet Dreams

Songs from the Shooting Gallery

DOWN AND OUT ON MURDER MILE

TONY O'NEILL

HARPER ● PERENNIAL

NEW YORK ● LONDON ● TORONTO ● SYDNEY ● NEW DELHI ● AUCKLAND

HARPER ● PERENNIAL

P.S.™ is a trademark of HarperCollins Publishers.

HarperCollins books may be purchased for educational, business, or sales promotional use. For information please write: Special Markets Department, HarperCollins Publishers, 10 East 53rd Street, New York, NY 10022.

FIRST EDITION

Drawing of warehouse and book design by Justin Dodd

Library of Congress Cataloging-in-Publication Data
    O'Neill, Tony.
      Down and out on murder mile / Tony O'Neill.—
  1st Harper Perennial ed.
      p.   cm.
  ISBN 978-0-06-158286-8

08 09 10 11 12 OV/RRD 10 9 8 7 6 5 4 3 2 1

For Nico Estrella O'Neill

DOWN AND OUT ON MURDER MILE

1

THEY GO TOGETHER LIKE A HORSE AND CARRIAGE

The first time I met Susan she overdosed on a combination of Valium and Ecstasy at a friend's birthday party at a Motel 6 on Hollywood Boulevard. My friends Sal, RP, and I dragged her blue face down to the 5:00 A.M. Hollywood streets below, and the filthy predawn drizzle on her face somehow brought her round. She blinked up at us and said: "I need a beer. And I want to shoot some pool."

I married her six months later. I had one broken marriage, one broken musical career, and a burgeoning heroin habit to contend with. I had nowhere I wanted to be, and neither did she. Without a strong pull in any other direction we decided to go down together.

————

I married my second wife the day the dissolution of marriage from the first disaster became final: we did it in the home of a Dominican notary public near Koreatown, having shot the last of our heroin and furiously smoked the last of the crack in the car parked outside. I was twenty-one years old.

Before the wedding we stopped at the storefront needle exchange on Cahuenga between Hollywood and Sunset. I wore a suit that had a few bloodstains on it and Susan wore a crumpled white dress. We dressed like that because the whole thing seemed slightly perverse to start off with, so why not go all out? Inside we received a few sideways glances, but nothing more. Needle exchanges are like porno bookstores or public toilets. Nobody wants to talk or even make eye contact unless it is absolutely necessary. The exchange had a front room where you could watch TV or get access to the Internet, as well as a table you could pick up lube and condoms at. I suppose that must have been for the meth freaks. In the back was a desk with a flip-top container for people to dump used needles into, and a storeroom full of syringes of all shapes and sizes. We used the standard Terumo 28 gauge ½ cc insulin needles because we were new at this and our veins were not too screwed up yet. We had not yet begun to inject into our groins, necks, or the backs of our knees. But there was still time.

Todd was a dreadlocked ex-junkie who worked the exchange on Wednesdays. He had been in Narcotics Anonymous for almost ten years. He was a good guy, one of the few people I knew in recovery who still gave a shit and tried to help those still strung out in a practical way. He doled out needles and advice every week for four hours on a strictly volunteer basis. He eyed us up and down as we dumped the old needles and requested a new hundred-count box.

"What's with the outfits?" He half smiled. "You two getting married or something?"

"Yup. We're on out way there now."

"Yeah." Todd sighed, sliding the box across to us, "Well, you know, congratulations."

My wife-to-be was a heroin-addicted thirty-two-year-old accountant. We married to keep me in the country as we were having such a good time getting high together. Meeting Susan was the moment that my drug use ceased to be a healthy product of my youth and recklessness and started to become the only thing that mattered to me. That old, drunken Irish fatalism that had been with me throughout my life suddenly resurfaced, and it was no longer enough to be high and having a good time. I needed to be higher. I needed to feel my heart pounding so hard it seemed as if it might burst loose from my ribcage. I needed to feel the palpitations and see my vision blurring, doubling. I needed to know that Death was here, in the room, and that I was too fast, too young, and too smart for him.

In the beginning we drove around in her eggshell-blue eighties Mercedes with the top rolled down, blasting punk rock from her tape player and pulling over to get high. We always had enough drugs. Heroin. Crack. Methamphetamine. We woke up and did drugs. We did drugs until we passed out. And the money was always there, the money I made writing music videos and the money she had saved from accounting jobs. The money would never run out, it seemed. And for her dollars, Susan had bought someone as completely into the idea of total destruction as she. It wasn't love, but there was the unspoken agreement that we would eventually die together.

The wedding was as brief and perfunctory as one could imagine. The house was a dimly lit, ramshackle little place. We signed the papers, high and twitchy, and since we didn't have any friends the old woman called her daughter, or her granddaughter, downstairs to act as witness. She was around sixteen years old and pissed off about being dragged away from her TV shows. She looked at us, silently chewing gum, and we shot back big stoned smiles at her. The whole thing was over in minutes. This now marked the second time that I had married someone while I was out of my mind on drugs. The first time was a rush job in Vegas to a vengeful blonde while ripped on booze and crystal meth. And now here, two years later, junked out of my brain and spun from smoking crack. I started singing Wagner's "Bridal Chorus" as we staggered out of the place and back into Susan's car.

We were renting a place in one of the poorer parts of Hollywood, a shabby building populated with burned-out drinkers and stoic old Armenian women. We moved in and never unpacked, so everything sat in cardboard boxes. The furniture that Susan had kept from her last divorce was stacked up in one corner, giving the apartment the look of someplace completely uninhabited by the living. The shades were drawn all day long. The only furniture we ever used was the couch, the coffee table where we divided the drugs, the television, and the filthy bed that we lay in moaning and cursing whenever the smack ran out.

Later that night, back at the apartment, we had our first married argument. We had miscalculated what was left in the bank, and the ATM refused to dispense cash. We had to wait for Susan's pay to arrive in two days. A phony check we deposited earlier hadn't cleared yet. There weren't enough drugs to get through the night and the only dealer who would take our calls was an evil little rat bastard called Raphael.

He agreed at first, but when he showed up to the place he was drunk and feeling mean.

"I no have no chiva," he kept telling us, "I don' know why you call me. Who are you?"

Susan turned to me and whispered, "He's drunk out of his fucking mind."

"Okay, okay," he yelled. "How much you wan?"

"Eighty?" Susan asked, rather optimistically.

"Okay. Where the money?"

———

"We won't have it until tomorrow! You said you'd give us credit!"

"I don' say nothing! I ain't Wells Fargo bitch! I no give no fucking loans!"

Then he pulled out his cell phone, furiously dialed a number, and started yelling at someone in Spanish.

"We're fucked!" Susan said, desperation creeping into her voice. "He ain't gonna play. We're gonna be sick again."

I cursed and started hunting around the place for electronics or jewelry that he might take in exchange for a bag of dope. But everything was already given away or in the pawn shop: the DVD player, the DVDs, the PlayStation, the CD player, my musical equipment, all gone. All we had was a busted TV and the cell phone, but without the phone we would be completely cut off. I returned from the bedroom, empty-handed, to find Susan in tears, screaming: "But it's my WEDDING DAY, asshole! You're crazy!"
"Hey hey!" I yelled. "Calm down!" Then, grabbing her by the arm, "Shit, cool it Susan! We're trying to get drugs out of him, not piss him off more!"

"He wants me to blow him," she snarled, "for the drugs. He wants me to suck his dick!"

"Oh."

I couldn't see the problem. Susan had sucked a lot of dick for drugs, for better grades, for promotions at work, or because some crazy pulled a knife and told her he'd gut her like a motherfucking pig if she didn't. I didn't assume that was going to stop because we had gotten married.

"Okay, I go. No time for this!" Raphael yelled.

"It's my *wedding day*!" Susan said again, drawing out the syllables until they bled.

"Well." I sighed. "It's up to you. Whatever you want."

"He fucking *stinks*!" she whispered. "And what if he doesn't give us the drugs afterward?"

"She wants the drugs first!" I yelled at him.

"No. They're in the car. I bring them after she keeps her part of the deal."

"That's it, Raphael. Fuck off!" she yelled, and he stormed out, dramatically slamming the door.

I couldn't help but believe in that optimistic dope-fiending part of my brain that if she had only sucked his dick for a few minutes, we would have had drugs. We didn't fight about that, though. When we started to get sick that night, we fought because we had spent our last fifty dollars on the wedding license instead of on heroin.

———

"I didn't know it was our last fifty bucks!" Susan pleaded.

"Well, that's great," I spat. "Some fucking accountant you are!"

At midnight we managed to get hold of Carlos, one of our back-up guys. He agreed to front us two bags until the next day. We drove down to Bonnie Brae and Sixth with a wastepaper basket on my lap for us to vomit into without having to pull over. The whole deal was extremely sketchy as on Wednesdays the cops had started to do sweeps of the area to bust junkies as they were leaving. Anyone who wasn't from the 90 percent Hispanic neighborhood was likely to get pulled over and questioned. Especially a white guy and a half-Chinese woman driving a Mercedes and vomiting into a trash can. Somehow we avoided a bust. We sailed right past a prowl car as they pulled some other poor bastard's car apart on Sixth Street.

On the way home we stopped at a McDonald's so we could go shoot up in the toilets. It was two in the morning and the only people in there were other junkies, street people, and the unfortunate teenagers working there. They played the Disney song "It's a Small World" at full volume, and they even piped it into the fucking toilet stall where I was fixing my dope.

And that's what happened the day I got married for the second time.

2

THIS IS WHAT KILLED HEMINGWAY

I suppose I could have been a doctor or an architect if I had devoted a quarter of the energy toward that as I did toward supporting my drug habit over the years. Maybe I could have painted masterpieces or cured cancer. But at the end of the day, the universe is finite, and soon everything mankind has achieved over the years will some day be gone. Even Leonardo da Vinci and Charles Darwin will one day be no more significant than a fossilized lump of dinosaur shit. Faced with that reality, getting high seems a hell of a lot more meaningful than trying to change the world.

Perfect, seasonless Los Angeles months passed, but neither of us seemed to notice. Susan somehow managed to hold down her job as the chief financial officer for a chain of Laundromats that operated all over Los Angeles County. She left for work each morning and left four syringes loaded with drugs for me—two dark brown shots of heroin and two light brown, potent speedballs—like a mother leaving her child a packed lunch.

Upon moving into the apartment neither of us bathed anymore. The bathroom lay pretty much unused, a symptom of both junkie constipation and poor hygiene. Garbage started to pile up, and Susan's cat, Hemingway, started to rip into and eat from the rancid garbage bags and drink from the dripping faucets out of desperation. The cat, as well as Susan and I, started to look mangy and ill. But without even heroin to mask the hunger pangs, Hemingway started to mewl and cry something awful all through the days and nights.

Susan used to talk about how much she loved the cat, and how heartbroken she was when its brother, Sartre, had died of leukemia. But now, if she heard the cat's cries at all, she never acknowledged them. He took to hiding away in the filth and the disarray, not even attempting to get our attention anymore. When the day came that I found him dead and starved, covered in his own watery shit and vomit under the kitchen sink, I didn't tell Susan. I threw his ruined body off the balcony for the coyotes to eat and kept my mouth shut. Susan never once inquired as to the whereabouts of her pet, and Hemingway's death remained my secret.

Susan ran her job into the ground pretty soon after. She would show up late and spend half her day locked in her office, with her feet on the desk and her tights around her knees, looking for working veins in her inner thighs and giving me protracted, blow-by-blow accounts of the whole process over the phone.

"Fuck . . . shit . . . it hurts like a motherfucker shooting here. . . . But I can't have track marks on my Goddamned hands anymore. . . . God-DAMN! Shit! Someone's knocking on the door! CONFERENCE CALL! BE WITH YOU IN FIFTEEN! Shit. . . . Argh, there's blood every-where. . . ."

Sometimes when she'd get the hit, she'd nod out right there on the phone with me. I'd listen to her softly breathing down the receiver before silently hanging up. Sweet dreams, Susan. I'd imagine what would happen on the day that someone finally opened her office door and found her, nod-ded out, slack-jawed, bloody legs splayed, with the syringe still sticking out of her groin and the phone wedged between her ear and her shoulder. Of course, the gig would be up soon, and Susan would be completely unemployable.

Pedro, my first dope connection, made the trip to our place only once. He reluctantly sold me the drugs and then spent an hour trying to convince me to quit.

"You're a fucking DEALER, Pedro! Why the fuck are you giving me this speech, man?"

"You're DYING, man! You an' this crazy whore you shacked up wit'! Ain't no dead junkie any use to me, man!"

———

He stopped returning my calls, even though I was into him for nearly $1,000 in credit. In a moment of phenomenal self-delusion I actually believed that he had cut me off because of his concerns for my health and well-being. Then I heard on the grapevine that he'd had a coke-induced stroke at the grand old age of twenty-nine. He survived, but the INS deported him as soon as he shuffled out of the hospital.

The job, the car, and the apartment all vanished in quick succession. Notice to quit the apartment appeared pinned to our front door because of the unpaid rent the day after the Laundromat canned Susan. When the notice appeared she seemed strangely relieved.

"Listen, we have to get out of here anyway."
"What? Why?"

"I think the cops are gonna be looking for me, and soon."

"The cops? What the fuck happened?"

"I stole from the company. A lot . . ." She looked like she was about to cry.

"How much?"

"A lot."

"Thousands?"

———

"Uh-huh."

"Like what? Five? Ten?"

Quietly she said, "Fifteen, at least."

We both sat in silence for a moment.

"Well . . . that's great. Shit! Where's the money! Let's split!"

"It's gone."

"What? Gone where?"

"We spent it all, asshole! On fucking drugs! How much do you think I made doing the books for a fucking Laundromat? We're broke!"

"Shit."

"Yup. We're fucked. Where are we gonna go?"

"Shit, Susan. I don't know anymore."

That Saturday night we had been up for almost forty-eight hours smoking crack and shooting speedballs. Half insane, I suddenly heard cop cars pulling up outside. We turned all of the lights out and the cop cars' flashing lights illuminated the apartment with an eerie, rhythmic glow. My guts flipped in fear.

"They're coming for us!" I whispered.

———

"The closet!"

We ran, shut ourselves in the closet, and sat in the dark, trying to smoke up the rest of the crack before the police broke the door down. Under a pile of clothes I found a flashlight and, balancing it in the crook of my neck, I tried to shoot some cocaine. My hands were shaking, the beam of light was unsteady, and I succeeded in tearing a big bloody hole in my arm and spraying blood all over the inside of the doors and our clothes. After half an hour, it all seemed quiet.

"Are they waiting for us?" I whispered.

"I don't know," Susan replied, her eyes wide with fear. "Maybe they're waiting for the feds to show up."

"Or the INS. Or Jesus! Are there any rocks left?"

Another ten minutes—or it could have been an hour—dragged past before I worked up the nerve to open the closet door and sneak over to take a look out the window. Outside the lights were still flashing, and I could hear voices. I peered through a crack in the blinds.

"Oh shit! Look at this!"

Susan crept out to the window in time to see her car being towed off down the street.

"Motherfuckers!" She groaned. "My fucking car!"

———

The glove compartment has been stuffed with outstanding tickets. The plates were expired too, and one night, insane with cocaine, I had removed the plates from a car parked farther down the street and stuck them to our bumper. They had obviously reported it, and the city took the car. We were officially fucked.

There was no place left to run. We called Susan's mother and told her what was happening. We asked to stay in her guesthouse for a while so we could clean up. Susan's mother was in a cult called the Forum and was an all-around nut. The whole family was pretty insane, but her mother was something else. She lived in Ghost Town, one of the worst slums in Venice. Going there to clean up was as ludicrous as moving to Vegas because you have a gambling problem. But it was a roof, and a place to stay for a few weeks. It was about then that I started thinking about getting away from Susan, and Los Angeles altogether. But then I looked at her, jobless, homeless, and hopeless, covered in dried blood and rocking back and forth on her heels whining to herself in insane, cracked-out fear, and I realized that for the time being I was stuck with her. I mean, I had encouraged her into this habit. Walking away at this point would have been tantamount to murder. The last time she tried to kill herself, she fucked it up, cut her wrists the wrong way, and lost the feeling in her pinkie fingers. I knew that the next time she wouldn't take any half measures. My only consolation was that at least the guns were in the pawnshop, for the time being.

I knew I had to make a break from Susan too. I knew I couldn't quit with her around, because there would always be one of us giving the other a reason to use again. I looked at her with a kind of mounting horror. My wife of six months was a skeletal, deathly figure. I'd wake up to find her trying to shoot dope into the little veins on the sides of her blood-dripping tits, a cigarette clamped between her shaking teeth. The party had stopped being fun sometime before we had married, and now it seemed like the only way out was death. I had never been as strung out as I was now. If I waited six hours in between hits, I would get sick. I woke up sick in the morning if I slept too long. If the heroin was there, I'd leave a loaded syringe by my bedside so I could fix before I was even fully awake.

The first reason I stayed with Susan was pity. She had had a horrible time of it before I came along. Her grandfather had plied her with booze and raped her when she was a teenager. The way Susan related the story, when she returned home sobbing and hysterical, Mommy didn't seem too bothered about the whole thing.

"Well, I did warn you about this," she told her. "You know he's into that kind of shit. I told you what he did to me when I was your age."

"What?" Susan sobbed. "Told me WHAT? YOU DIDN'T TELL ME ANYTHING!"

"Oh," her mother replied. "Maybe it was your sister I talked to. Anyway . . . you'll get over it. I did."

———

After that trauma there was a host of others. Rapes. Beatings. It all sounded too outrageous, too Gothic to be made up. Who makes that kind of shit up? At the time, I was shocked and began to feel very protective toward her. Only later did I realize that among female junkies Susan was no exception. All of the females I have come into contact with on the scene had similar stories. Rape. Child abuse. Incest. Female addicts predominantly are a certain type and that type— sadly—is the used and the abused.

Also, my perception of myself started to change. I faced it every morning in the filthy mirror: I was an intravenous heroin user, out of necessity a thief and a scam artist. My looks where shot to hell, my arms were open sores, and my teeth were falling out of my head. I was turning into some horrible mirror image of Susan. I felt as if I had taken so many steps into a maze that I could no longer retrace them and find my way back to the start. I had no option but to keep going and to pray that I would chance upon a chink of sunlight. I was lost, lost, lost, and could find sustenance only in drugs and our encroaching despair.

It was now Christmas Eve. We had twenty dollars left. We had started up on crack early that evening and now the money was gone and we were in trouble. Twenty dollars' worth of crack is nothing once you've taken your first hit already. It won't even sustain you. It will delay the crash for maybe ten minutes. Try and split a twenty-dollar rock in two and you may as well light the bill itself and try and get high off the fumes. It was 11:00 P.M. Susan was on my last fucking nerve, begging and wheedling and pushing me to go out and score more crack.

"I'm not going out there," I told her, "That's it. At least we have twenty bucks for tomorrow. The place is crawling with pigs. Everyone is drunk and high and crazy. Anyway, it's Christmas Eve for chrissakes. All of the dealers are gonna be back home. The only people out there are gonna be scam artists looking to rip off stupid white kids out trying to score."

She was cleaning out the pipe, trying to find a grain of residue that she had missed on the previous five rounds of cleaning the pipe. The pipe was clean as it could be. It was gleaming. I knew it was futile. She knew it was futile. But she persisted in heating up the stem and using a piece of wire to drag the Brillo through the glass repeatedly, trying to pick up some melted cocaine.

"Then *I'll* go."

"You're not going."

"I'm gonna go. I'm a girl. They'll cut me a break."

"They'll cut your fucking throat after they're done gang-banging you," I told her. "Now don't be so fucking stupid. We're gonna need smack tomorrow. We ain't spending our last twenty bucks on a rock. It's over. Take some pills and go to sleep."

———

She continued to clean the pipe, holding it up to her lips for a futile attempt at smoking the residue, cursing, and getting back to work.

"You are a motherfucker," she told me matter-of-factly.

"And you're a fucking crackhead. You're out of your fucking mind. Now give it up."

She carried on scraping the pipe and tried to take another hit. Of course there was nothing. She started to cry, big heaving sobs like hot needles inserted into my nerve endings. Then she picked up one of my books, one of the big ones. Céline maybe, or a dictionary or a medical book. I don't remember. She held it in both of her hands, gripping it tightly until the knuckles turned white before she started to smash herself in the face with it, her sobs becoming more and more frenzied and grating. After the fourth or fifth *thump* I yelled at her to knock it off. I grabbed my keys.

"I'm going, you stupid cunt," I grumbled, "I won't be long."

The streets of Ghost Town were alive with junkies, dealers, and all kinds of human flotsam. Most of them were rip-off artists. On more than one occasion I had been sold soap or some other unpleasant-tasting shit instead of the crack I wanted. I retraced the steps I had taken earlier, hoping to locate the last guy I had bought off. I turned the corner and tried to locate the kid's spot.

I coughed and tried to draw attention to myself. The bastard popped up, right on cue: "Psst!"

We did the deal, and I split back for our place. Sirens provided constant background noise, as did the throbbing of helicopters circling overhead. It was like living in some grotesque, drugged-out *Blade Runner* hell. I was thinking this as I stepped off the curb and into the path of an LAPD patrol car, lights blazing, sirens roaring, and speeding toward me.

I had no time to react. I was bathed in light momentarily as my feet left the ground and my whole being shook. . . . I flipped back, weightless and graceful, a moment that seemed to stretch to infinity.

Crunch!

I couldn't even process the information until after I had bounced off the car's hood and back onto the tarmac with a yell of surprise. I looked up and saw two cops looking down on me, like angels of doom.

"You okay?" one of the cops asked.

"Yeah," I said, getting to my feet gingerly.

The other cop radioed in to the station as I started to feel warm blood trickling down my left leg. "You just stepped out," the cop nearest me—a virtual man mountain with a buzz cut—told me. "We couldn't stop. We were in pursuit. Didn't you hear the sirens?"

———

Well, of course I heard the sirens, but I'd heard them so often all night that I had begun to block them out like all of the other city noise. I was concentrating more on getting me—and the crack—back indoors.

Oh Jesus. The crack! My stomach began to churn and fear welled up inside me. I started to talk fast.

"You know I wasn't concentrating on what I was doing. Preoccupied. Completely my fault, I'm really sorry."

"What are you doing out here? This isn't a good neighborhood."

"I live right down there. I'm on my way home."

"Well, we're gonna radio for an ambulance to have you checked out."

"No need!" I insisted. "I'm fine. Listen, my wife is at home, she's gonna freak out if I'm not back in twenty minutes. You know how it is in this neighborhood. I'd rather just go home and forget about it."

The cops eyed me for a while. It was quite obvious to them that I was half out of my mind on drugs. It was also obvious that I could create a bunch of paperwork for them if I went to the hospital because they hit me while I crossed the road. They didn't want the paperwork and I didn't want to have my pockets turned out.

"Well," said the cop with the buzz cut, "if you're sure you're all right. . . ."

"Positive." I beamed. "Never better! Happy Christmas officers!"

"Yeah, you too," they growled, getting back into their car.

I limped back into the guesthouse. I sat down and rolled up my pant leg, exposing a large ugly gash running up my shin.

"Jesus!" Susan said, coming over to look. "What happened?"

"I got knocked over by a cop car. They let me go. I told you it's a fucking mess out there tonight. I should have never gone . . . Fuck!"

I went to the bathroom and peeled off my bloody jeans, trying to wash the dirt out of the wound as best I could. Susan popped her head in the door after a few minutes.

"You could have been busted," she said, quietly.

"I know. Or killed. Imagine that. Killed on Christmas Eve by a speeding cop car. Jesus!"

———

Susan smiled a little and said, "Pretty funny, huh?"

I just glowered at her.

"No," I told her eventually. "Not really."

"Did you get the rock?"

I sighed and nodded toward the bloody jeans. She retrieved it and scuttled out of the room.

I got cleaned up and found her playing with the pipe, exhaling white smoke. I limped over and said, "Where's mine?" She handed me the pipe. I held the lighter up and took a long drag. Nothing. Not even a glimmer of something.

"Where's the rest?" I asked her. "You killed this one."
"That's it."

"That's it?"

"Yeah . . . it was a small rock. That's it."

"Well thanks," I told her. "That's fucking great. Thank you so fucking much."

"Don't yell at me!" she said, before adding quietly "It *is* Christmas, you know."

I looked at the clock. Ten after midnight. Well, she was right about something. It was Christmas.

I looked out of the window and could see nothing but vast, endless black. Somewhere out there was the moon and the stars and the Pacific Ocean, but from where I was looking I could have been a thousand feet underground. I could hear her, somewhere behind me, starting to nervously clean out the pipe again. It would be less than an hour before she started up again, maybe two before she started bashing herself in the face with my books and sobbing. But for now, for a moment, there was peace on earth.

4

HOMECOMING

Airports hold a special sense of horror for me. They rank in my top five least favorite places in the world. They are especially awful if seven days ago you kicked heroin cold turkey in a shithole motel called the Deville—you and your junkie wife puking into the toilet, the sink, the shower, watching reruns of *The Golden Girls* and *Judge Judy,* curled into agonized balls in opposite corners of the room, masturbating and crying to pass the time.

Airports rank alongside the post-OD ride in an ambulance, pumped full of the Narcan that has ripped you from the mouth of endless white light and deposited you into that instant, chemically induced cold turkey so severe they had to strap you down to the gurney. Airports rank alongside the East LA crack house where, at seven in the morning when the money and the rock have run out, you sat twitching with a bunch of coke-crazed lunatics, terrified to exit into the unforgiving LA sunlight and figure out just what the fuck you are gonna do now, hopelessly combing the filthy carpet for a rock of crack you are convinced you must have dropped earlier in the session.

I find airports THAT awful.

It's the brightness and the sterility of them. The way everyone looks so fucking STRAIGHT and HEALTHY, like they have never so much as experienced a minute as awful and degenerate as your last year has been. The insinuating way the airport security staff talks to you and look at you: like they KNOW you're up to something. It's almost like they think they are doing you a favor by letting you travel to another country. The unspoken question of "Why should we let a scumbag like YOU cross international borders?"

That edge of twitchy paranoia is increased a thousandfold when you feel as raw and as fucked up as I felt that day, preparing to return to London from Los Angeles. Out of options, we had decided to flee to England's friendlier climes. At least there we could receive treatment for our addiction. In the United States we were thrown to the lions: even the "free" methadone clinic on Hollywood Boulevard expected its clients to show up with twelve dollars a day, for each dose of methadone. When heroin is only seven dollars a bag downtown, and the clinic won't even provide enough methadone to keep you out of withdrawal . . . well, you can do the math. Susan's mother was eager to see us leave the United States, even paid for our plane tickets. Susan and I were convinced the airport cops were gonna pounce on us before we even made it to the plane.

"There the bastards are!" they'd yell. *"Trying to skip the country!"*

They'd hold us down and read the litany of crimes: my being in the country illegally for over a year. Possession and use of controlled substances. Thousands of dollars in bounced checks, ripped bank accounts, unpaid rent. The $15,000 stolen from Susan's old job. Maybe they'd even show up with every heroin and crack dealer we still owed money to in LA, for a bit of summary street justice. That bill alone had to amount to tens of thousands of dollars—double, triple the amount worth killing us for. Holy fuck, the sweat was running off me as I handed my passport over. Dripping from my nose. Soaking through my shirt and onto the crumpled suit I wore in an attempt to look inconspicuous. Only the suit was red sharkskin and had dark bloodspots on the trousers from shooting up. I don't think it had ever been cleaned since I bought it, high on crack, a year ago. I was the most conspicuous person in the airport, almost comically noticeable.

"You have nothing on you," I told myself. "Calm the fuck down."

"But wait," my paranoia piped up. *"You packed in a hurry. What if you left something in your clothes by mistake? A balloon? A rock? An old syringe?*

And do you really trust that junkie bitch? What if she slipped something in YOUR luggage? She's done dumber things! They have sniffer dogs ... X-rays.... They'll bust you before you can get out. You'll never leave this fucking city. It WANTS you. In a crack house or in a prison cell; doesn't matter: it'll HAVE you."

I bought a book waiting for our flight to be called. Why the fuck didn't we score some smack before we left? One balloon to make the flight bearable? Bullshit bravado, that's all it was. We were terminal fools. The book was a trashy paperback about—what else?—a couple who sinks into heroin addiction. I figured it would pass the eleven hours until I hit London.

We made it onto the plane. Right up until take-off I expected the pigs to rush onto the plane and bundle us off. The pilot to announce: *"Ladies and gentlemen . . . do not panic. We have fugitives on board and they are about to be removed.... Do not interfere with the apprehension of the suspects."*

When the plane picked up speed on the runway I had the sense of the Devil itself chasing the jet, snarling and slobbering and snapping in frustration as we climbed just out of reach. The sky, though, provided no sanctuary from my toxic thoughts.

The fat American businessman next to me took up half of my seat as well as his own. Susan was anxiously looking out the window. Even with her hair washed and clean clothes on, she looked like a junkie whore. Aw Jesus, I had to tell my parents that I was married again. This time to a fucking junkie! The crash from the cocaine was dwindling to a throbbing sleep-deprived headache and the relentless hum of post-heroin-withdrawal anguish was returning, as I knew it would.

Jesus, it was hot.

Aren't planes supposed to be air-conditioned? I tried to get comfortable but either hit Susan's bony elbow if I moved too far left or the businessman's hammy arm if I slithered too far to the right. My squirming and jostling for position was obviously irritating him. He stared at me, round and pink and disgusted for a moment, before returning his attention to some banal magazine aimed at men. Cars. Gadgets. Women with big tits and white smiles. A world as alien to me as that of ecosystems at the bottom of the ocean. I smelled. I smelled like a man who had been shitting and vomiting and sweating out the heroin for a week and cleaned himself quickly in the sink of a motel with a ratty-looking washcloth before he left for the airport. I smelled like a man whose last act before leaving that dark cave was to take one final hit from the pipe and watch his face carefully in the mirror as he exhaled plumes of white smoke, while a cab honked outside in the parking lot. A man who had vaguely considered just staying there and trying to rustle up more credit for crack, just stay in that room and just *be*. To simply wait until the cops or death came and put an end to the whole sorry mess.

———

He cleared his throat, irritated. The fat pig was irritated by my presence. This tub of fucking lard that was taking up half of my Goddamned seat with his flab—flab no doubt put on over expensive business lunches and good brandy—was irritated by me! Self-righteous anger bubbled up inside of me.

Who was the real monster? M or this self-important cocksucker? This businessman? This evil corporate dick-sucking bastard? WHO WAS THE REAL MONSTER?

Calm down. Breathe. You're crazy right now—you're sick. Keep it together. Order a drink and shut the fuck up for the next eleven hours. You need to make it home without getting arrested.

Suspended somewhere in the sky I sat in the tiny toilet and looked at myself. I looked as if I hadn't slept in years. I jerked off quickly and brutally—it was over in seconds, one of the odder effects of heroin withdrawal. The climax sent a small rush of serotonin to my brain, giving me relief for a few seconds at least. I knew in a few hours I was going to arrive at Manchester airport to see my parents for the first time in over a year. Then I was going to return to London in an attempt to somehow insinuate myself back into the music industry. Beyond that, I had planned nothing. Especially here, absurdly suspended in a toilet thousands of feet in the air, I knew the idea was ridiculous. I wondered vaguely how long it would be before I fucked up again.

———

Someone rapped on the door, agitated.

"How long you gonna be in there?"

I stood up and washed my hands.

"Not long," I replied.

5

JANUARY

We hit London with two thousand pounds and a
bank account with an overdraft limit of a thousand. We had spent a few weeks in Blackburn
with my parents trying to get ourselves oriented.
The town was much as I remembered it when
I left and never looked back at seventeen years
old—small, dull, and entirely without charm.
It was just another one of the increasingly ghet-
toized towns on the outskirts of Manchester that
stagnated without any effective rail links to the
big city to sustain any kind of cultural exchange.
Life in Blackburn was insular and suspicious.
The only entertainment on offer was a crumbling
cinema in the center of town with four screens
and sticky brown carpets from the mid-seventies
and the endless succession of pubs and clubs in
which the townsfolk drank and drank until they
collapsed, vomiting, into the gutters.

———

The money came from my parents, who desperately wanted me to get on my feet. The first two days at my childhood house we were too sick and too depressed to talk to them. The shock of my sudden return, coupled with the appearance of a new wife, must have nearly killed them. They had a vague idea that I was using drugs, but when I staggered off the plane, still sick and unsteady and with a thirty-two-year-old wife—who looked at least ten years older—in tow, all of their worst fears must have been confirmed with interest. Susan at least made the effort to cover her track marks with makeup, but succeeded only in making herself look like a burn victim. I had to remind her to wear trousers or jeans at all times, because her legs were such a fucking mess. We both looked like the ideal "Just Say No" poster children.

Feigning jetlag, I slept the days away with the curtains drawn, emerging only to eat, stare at the television, and return to my room. Awake at three in the morning in the silent house, I fretted that I would never have the strength to emerge and talk to them. I stood at their door and listened to their frenzied whispers and my mother's stifled sobs. I also knew that I would eventually have to, in order to get back to London, where at least I would be granted the anonymity I so desperately needed right now. I crept down the stairs and into the darkened kitchen to get some water. I still felt like shit. I wondered vaguely if I could find some heroin in Blackburn. I had looked at the local paper, the *Lancashire Telegraph,* for stories on drugs and found mention of a few arrests of heroin dealers. I knew then that it was around. But I also knew that in a town as parochial and shut off as this one I would have a hard time scoring from people I didn't know. Nobody just shows up in a place like Blackburn from out of town and tries to connect for drugs—they grow up here, stay here, work the same dead-end jobs for years here, and buy drugs from the same small-town, small-time drug dealers.

Rifling through the drawers in the kitchen I found one drawer full of various medicines. I had, of course, already made the medicine cabinet in the bathroom for drugs, but found nothing. Here too it looked like I would be similarly disappointed: nothing but a lot of over-the-counter remedies for everything from sleeplessness to upset stomachs. The few prescription bottles in there were mostly blood pressure related. Then I came across a plain white box with a green-and-white prescription label affixed dead center.

"Dihydrocodeine Tartrate," the label read, "30 mg. Take one to two tablets for moderate to severe pain."

They were meant for my father's arthritis. He had a phobia of doctors and medication though, and obviously had never even so much as opened the box. The label dated the pills to July 2000. All one hundred tablets where still encased in their foil blister packs.

"Thank you," I whispered to the God who watches over junkies and fuckups.

———

I slept that night with the box under my pillow, feeling like a child with its favorite teddy bear. For once my sleep was relatively peaceful. The dreams still persisted, of course, how could they not? But when I jerked awake, I slid my hand under the pillow and felt the comforting smoothness of the box of tablets and was asleep again, almost instantly. I wondered about keeping the box a secret from Susan, but I knew that she would sniff out the fact that I was high immediately. Unfortunately I would have to split the drugs with her.

The next morning I was all business. I went downstairs and took my first three tablets with a cup of coffee. I was long enough off heroin that even 90 mg of dihydrocodeine—something that would previously not have even stopped my nose from running—now gave me a pleasant, woozy kind of high. I shaved, brushed my teeth, and showered for the first time since I had arrived in Blackburn. Then I set about the careful business of convincing my parents—and myself—that everything was all right, and that Susan and I needed to get to London to kick-start my ailing career. Of course, for the move I would need some kind of capital, a loan maybe, and then I could start getting it together and finally make them proud of me.

I could see it in their eyes: *He seems so happy. He seems at peace. He seems to have a plan.*

Our flame-out in Los Angeles became the subject that dare not speak its name. I ran errands with my mother, had drinks with my father at the barfly joint he hung out at every night at the end of their street, my jangling nerves coated with opiates. It was there I realized why I could never be anything but a junkie anymore. *It's only when I'm on opiates,* I reasoned, *that I know how to act like a normal human being. Like a normal son.*

"Why don't you stay here for a while?" my father asked over his pint of bitter in the Stop and Rest, while around us the old drinkers coughed phlegmy coughs and smoked and laughed.
"There's nothing for me here, Dad," I told him as gently as possible, "You know that."
"I know," he said sadly, "Sure there's nothing here for anybody. . . ."

That was true. Looking around the pub, the smell of decay was palpable: the yellow-stained ceiling and walls, the faded and ruined 1960s carpeting, the single, lonely fruit machine, the air thick with smoke from cheap cigarettes. There was no attempt to create a pleasant atmosphere to drink in. This was a working-class drinker's pub, nothing here but alcohol and a smattering of other boozers. It was hard to say how a pub so small still managed to look so empty and so sad, but this place managed both of those things. It reminded me in atmosphere of the crack houses dotted around MacArthur Park that I once frequented—the same lonely, furtive atmosphere— the same sense that this was a place for achieving oblivion, nothing more.

The clientele was almost entirely male (apart from the pudgy, big-permed barmaid) and mostly made up of cirrhotic old men. Even the young people who sometimes came in looked prematurely old—they looked worn out, ashen, and used up: ground down into premature agedness by lifetimes of boredom, booze, and drudgery. The smell of Sunday afternoons, gray skies, stifling hours dragging by in dusty sitting rooms and parlors. The place was a museum of soul-death by inertia.

Once I had secured the loan from my parents, I went to the bank to get an account. I figured that having been out of the country for so long and having no real credit history I'd be lucky to get a checkbook. However, when I was taken into the room to fill out the paperwork I lucked out and ended up with a young, hyperactive closet queen as my advisor. When he asked about my lack of a work history and I told him I had just returned from LA his eyes lit up.

"Oh," he said, "I've always wanted to visit America. What were you doing over there?"

"Writing music videos."

"Really?" he gasped, "How glamorous. Why on earth did you come back here?"

"Well," I told him, "I wanted to get back into playing music. My old band was pretty big here but no one had heard of us in the States. So I decided to come back to where people remembered us. You remember the Catsuits?"

———

"Oh yeah—I have a few singles of theirs!"

"Well, that was my band."

And that was all it took. I played the big music star returning from Los Angeles, and this idiot lapped it all up. It was that easy. Every time the computer flashed up LOAN RISK!!! in big flashing red letters he just muttered, "Okay, we can bypass this . . ." and clicked a button. In thirty minutes I had a checkbook and a bank card with an overdraft. I made up stories of seeing celebrities at fictitious restaurants in Beverly Hills and the poor sap bought it all. When I was done and the guy approved me, I walked over to the train station and bought a ticket for London Euston: it was that simple. I had a sense that once I hit the capital, everything would be all right. I popped some more painkillers and stopped at one of the dozens of bars dotted around the station to get a drink. Things were finally coming together.

6

RJ

Upon hitting London, we checked into a cheap, damp,
shabbily furnished room in a Russell Square
hotel. We simply arrived in Euston with our cases
and checked into the cheapest rooming house we
could find. The place was populated by backpacking students and drunken Australians who
lounged around in the communal areas drinking
cans of Foster's and Tennent's, smoking joints,
and watching daytime television.

The only contact with other human beings we
had was in twelve-step meetings around the
city, where we sat in silence and listened to other
people's stories. We did not go in an attempt to
stay clean. More than anything, I wanted to score
drugs. I convinced Susan it would be a smart idea
to attend. I was so out of touch with the London
scene that I got ripped off the first few times I

attempted to buy from the street. One afternoon I found myself chased down Euston Road by a braying pack of Rastafarian crack dealers who took my money and sold me a piece of gum wrapped in a baggie. After I confronted them they pulled their gums back from their yellow teeth and actually howled and yelped like fucking wolves, before giving chase. I ran, gasping for air, knocked over an old hooker, and lost them by the McDonald's near the train station. Similar scenes repeated themselves a dozen times or more. Susan sat around the room, chain-smoking and depressed, and I would set out every morning—like a man attempting to look for gainful employment—in an attempt to make a connection for heroin.

Having never scored heroin in London, I assumed that the street-dealing scene would be identical to that of Los Angeles. That I would be able to walk up to any dealer, hand over my money, and walk away with drugs. Not so. If you wanted pills or hash or grass then it was readily available from the kids who loitered on Camden High Street after dark. But the heroin- and crack-dealing scenes where much more underground. Unbeknownst to me at the time, they were relegated to the "frontlines," open dealing spots dotted sparsely around the city. But if you were an outsider, you were an easy target for rip-off artists. When I walked up to these kids and asked for smack I was inevitably sold a wrap containing nothing. When I returned to complain, the dealer was gone, carried away on the scent of fat cooking on kebab skewers, piss, and the smoke from cheap blocks of hash.

———

I thought that Narcotics Anonymous meetings would be a good spot to get more information about where the real heroin and crack
scene was centered. Only it was tough to walk
right up to people who were in recovery and try
and get that kind of information. So we just sat
and listened, waiting for clues. I had patience.
I had nothing but time. I was an invisible man,
blended completely into the chaos of the capital.
After the meetings we returned to the rooming
house and sat with the blinds drawn, the dark
enveloping us, and we waited. I imagined that
if I concentrated hard enough I could disappear
completely.

Sometimes some well-meaning sort would offer
to buy us a coffee after the meeting. As with all
junkies in recovery, the talk was inevitably concentrated around drugs. The serenity and the
clean-living bullshit that everybody bandied
about in the meetings soon vanished into unre-
strained drug talk. Like men with no dicks talking about all the pussy they used to get.

"... and then I fixed the morphine drip in the hospital, so I could get enough out of it to stay high
on ..."

"... when they closed down the needle exchanges
in Glasgow I'd just fish the used needle bins out of
the Dumpsters at the hospital, get the old spikes
out, file 'em down, bleach 'em, and use 'em ...
only sometimes there was no time for filing and
bleaching ..."

———

". . . yeah the skag was so much better then. Little tablets we used to get . . . 'jacks' they called 'em . . . just cook 'em right down and shoot them . . ."

". . . and there I was, sick as shit on the cell floor, shitting my pants . . . screaming, and the guards wouldn't even call the fucking doctor . . ."

". . . when my cousin OD'd on that stuff we went and found his connection and bought as much of it as we could. You see, we knew it had to be good shit then. . . ."

". . . high as a cunt, I just picked up a two-thousand-quid rug from Harrods and walked straight out of the front door. I think they figured I was a delivery guy or something. I walked it straight to my fence and got two hundred quid for it. That was back when you could buy Diconal and Ritalin cheap in the West End. . . . Ever shoot Diconal? It's a better rush than heroin . . . hits you like a speedball. . . ."

" . . . you see this leg? Right here, below the knee, where it goes purple? It's a deep vein thrombosis. I got it shooting Palfium. They don't like to prescribe it anymore. Pink palfs . . . they were the best. Better than skag. You got to crush 'em up good and cold shake it in the syringe. But if you don't shake it well enough you fuck up your veins. Once I got this I was able to hit up doctors for pain pills better than ever. File a lost-and-found slip at the train station saying you left a bag containing pain meds on the train. Then call an emergency doctor at night and show 'em the slip and tell 'em you're in pain. Once the fuckers took a look at my leg they were always good for more pills until the doctor's office opened. Do it on a Friday and you could get enough to get loaded with for the whole weekend...."

I had come back to a city I no longer belonged to. Junkie and fuckup stuck out all over me like a warning sign to potential employers, friends, or lovers. I found myself unable to even relate to my old friends. I called up Emma from the Catsuits and found myself invited up to her place in Crouch End for a party. She lived with our old guitar player Marie, so this would be a reunion of sorts. I knew there would be a lot of old faces from my music days. Susan stayed alone in the hotel. I arrived early and nervously downed pints in an Irish theme pub across the road. I felt like an imposter, uncomfortably lurking in a sharkskin suit. I stood in the bathroom staring in the mirror trying to perfect looking normal, nonchalant. "Hey, how's it going?" I practiced saying.

At the party, the usual round of So-what-have-you-been-up-to?'s. Everybody looked pretty much the same, apart from me. Intensely aware of the lines under my eyes, the puffiness of my face, the track marks still healing on the backs of my hands. I drank too much, said too much. Got into an argument over politics with an earnest young *NME* journalist in the kitchen, secretly pissed that he was hogging the whiskey, and hating the fact he was wearing an 'ironic' Kylie Minogue T-shirt. I told him he was a know-nothing college-boy asshole. He was talking about Tony Blair,

picking sides, the same old arguments I always
heard at home.

"It doesn't matter," I told him, drunkenly leaning
in too close. "We're all dying. . . . Why do you *care*
what variety of shit you have to eat in the meantime?"

I drunkenly showed my track marks to Dante
Thomas, an old friend from the music days. His
band had been the most successful unsuccessful band in history. He looked identical to the
last time I had seen him, staring at my plate with
a head full of Ecstasy in the Stock Pot, Soho,
1998.
"My, my" he said. "Aren't you the reckless one. . . ."

All that Emma and Marie wanted to talk about was
the old days, the carefree days of my drinking and
fooling around as if the crash wouldn't happen.
Too much "remember when . . . ?" for my stomach.
I could sense I was disappointing them. I felt old
and tired and sad that I hadn't stayed here instead
of leaving. Maybe then I wouldn't have been so
worn out, so beat down by circumstance.

Eventually, I drank all of the red wine and whiskey in the place and left to try and score with a
sallow-looking guy who said he used smack once
in a while and knew where to get it, even at one in
the morning.

"You just got to look for prostitutes," he told
me. "Wherever the prostitutes are there will be
dealers. . . ."

———

Tried to get money but I was so drunk I forgot my PIN number. The guy got nervous that I was trying to hustle him out of money and split, leaving me stranded in north London. I tried to kick the screen on the ATM in, and fell over on the pavement with the piss and the rain and the mud.

After two unsuccessful weeks in the hostel we found a flat share advertised in a free paper. It was a two-bedroom council flat in a high-rise in Hammersmith. The place had the improbable address of 109 Batman Close, and cost one hundred pounds per week. It was close enough to the BBC's White City studios that when the Real IRA exploded a car bomb outside of there the day after we moved in, the windows of our room shook, and I thought that the walls were caving in around us literally as well as figuratively. Our flat mates were a couple, he a monstrous English beer belly constantly sucking on a joint, drinking lager, glued to *The Weakest Link* or *Bargain Hunt*. She was South African, tall with a butch buzz cut, piercings dangling from her face. We heard them fuck noisily and constantly through the walls of our bedroom, and I listened to the creaking and his grunting and her oh-oh-there-yeah-there-don't-stop's and watched the wet patch on the ceiling, with Susan sleeping beside me or threatening suicide and chain-smoking again. I listened to the Queens Park Rangers crowd roaring from the stadium across the road, daytime television dancing across my face. I knew that soon I would be insane or a suicide myself.

———

I really needed to score.

Then I came across RJ. I met him outside of the needle exchange on Fortress Road, Shepherds Bush. I had stumbled across the store-front needle exchange a week after arriving in Hammersmith, while wandering the area's backstreets. I went there under the cover of getting needles but with the real intention of talking to some local junkies. The place was deserted though, apart from the guys who worked there—a couple of older black ex-dopers. One guy took care of me while the other hung out watching TV, asked me to fill out a form, and I gave a false surname and address. He was polite, respectful. He noticed the trace of an accent I had picked up in LA and in true dope-fiend fashion asked me what the heroin was like on the West Coast.

I told him that since my return to London I had been smoking heroin but now I wanted to inject again. He filled me in on the need to cook down UK heroin in citric acid. He gave me a pack of forty insulin needles, packets of citric acid, cookers, filters, sterile water, alcohol swabs, and a bin for disposing old needles in. As I was finishing the paperwork I noticed a tall, gaunt figure ring the bell and get buzzed in. He moved quickly, with a junky's determination, dropping off his old needles and following the guy into the back room to pick up more. I thanked my guy and walked out, loitering by the front entrance to talk to the new arrival as he left.

———

"Hey, how's it going?" I asked as he walked out the door. He looked a little startled but stopped to answer me.

"Not bad, mate."

I got a closer look at him, yet could not get a read of his face. It was as if he was petrified in wax, his features out of focus and indistinct. He wore a cream winter sports jacket and baseball cap, but beyond these features I could not pinpoint anything distinct about him. If he changed his outfit he would have become completely unrecognizable to me.

"Listen man . . . I just moved here and I need to score, badly. I ain't a cop or anything. . . . Can you help me out?"

"Well," he told me, "I figure they ain't got Yanks workin' for the drug squad now. . . . Wass yer name, mate?"

We exchanged pleasantries and he told me his name was RJ.

"I can't do anyfing right now, but I can sort you out after six if yer like. You got a pen?"

And that was how it started again. We split with each other's mobile numbers and my lethargy and depression melted away with each successive step. I had three hours to kill. I sat in the McDonald's on Shepherds Bush Green nursing a Coke and watching council estate mums with

their hair pulled back in severe ponytails pushing red-faced screaming children, flabby white
arses peeking out of the tops of tracksuit bot-
toms. . . .

. . . An old homeless guy with shit stains on his
filthy wool suit walking the gray streets and rum-
maging through a garbage can looking for food . . .
quick-talking black kids with impenetrable West
London–Jamaican accents hanging on a fence,
slapping palms, wolf-whistling at the young
snatch as it walked by . . .

I returned to the flat beaming with pride. The
hunter who had returned with enough provisions
for the family. Susan even attempted a stilted,
awkward hug, and we sat and waited for six
o'clock to roll around.

That evening I established what was to become
my routine over the next few months. My mobile
phone buzzed to life and I answered it breath-
lessly after the first ring.

"It's RJ. I'm walkin' up on your place now. I'll be
there in a few minutes."

I slipped my shoes on, put on my leather jacket,
and crept out the front door. I exited the Stalinist-
gray block of flats and leaned by the door watching for RJ to appear from the background static
of the city. Kids played in the concrete and the
broken glass, one suspiciously poking at a dead
cat with a stick.

———

Cars dragged past the estate, their souped-up sound systems causing the windows in the flats and houses to vibrate in unison. The sky was a murky gray, already dark outside at six, dirty yellow streetlights bathing the moist fog in an eerie glow. Then RJ would appear, sometimes on time, sometimes late, but always with that lurching, determined walk, winking at me—"All right, mate?"—as we both slipped into the block of flats.

We always did business in the piss-filled elevator, both of us red-cheeked and wet-nosed from the London winter. I had the money counted out, and he spat the wrap out and handed it to me. When we reached the third floor I got out, said good-bye, and RJ headed back down to the street and more deliveries.

We saw RJ through London winters and London summers. Through dry spells when we were all scrabbling and sick, not enough dope to keep everybody well, and through times of plenty. Good cheap heroin and plenty of it—wars and surplus—small white bags, spat from his mouth into his palm, and into my palm and into my mouth, the Kings Mall, Hammersmith, the piss and bleach of the stairs and the cold that penetrated the concrete façade, and home: Baggies untied, ripped open, tan powder dumped into spoons and the sickly sweet smell of cooking junk and peace. . . . Endless, terrible, beautiful peace. Sometimes he would show with his brother Mike, a tall skinhead with a mean look but who was actually one of the most harmless, sweet guys you could hope to meet. They were both addicts. I had the sense that RJ looked after Mike and made sure that he got by day to day.

Back in my room I locked the door and threw my coat on the bed. Susan looked up expectantly as I walked in and whispered, "Got it!"

With shaking cold hands I unwrapped the white plastic package and poured out its contents onto a CD case. I felt a familiar excitement rising in my chest. There it was, heroin, the first heroin I had had since Los Angeles. It was a light tan-colored powder and after being off for so long it seemed like a surprisingly large amount. I briefly considered the possibility that getting high might not be such a smart idea, but the thought was ludicrous and abstract now that the heroin was here in front of me. Up until this moment I had constantly been searching for it, and always in the back of my mind thinking that if it didn't present itself to me then that was it—it was meant to be, I was to remain clean. But if it fell into my lap, then it was meant to be also. I should use again. This Zen attitude toward using heroin was negated somewhat by the fact that I had spent nearly every day since arriving in London trying to score heroin. I had sought it out, and when a junkie puts out the distress signal that he needs junk in a big city, somebody somewhere will respond. It was no accident that I found myself in a locked bedroom with a bag of disposable needles and twenty pounds of heroin—it was the only possible conclusion to my repeated attempts at scoring. However, the idea that fate had presented me with this opportunity to get high made me feel slightly better about myself as I prepared my first shot, slid the fresh needle into my buttock, and injected into the fat and muscle there. After all, you don't want to fuck with fate, right?

When we were done I tidied my equipment away and walked out into the main room, leaving Susan alone with her high on the bed. My room-mate was sitting there, drinking a can of Stella and watching some obnoxious TV show at a brutal volume.

"All right?" he said. "Didn't hear you come in."

I sat in silence for a while and watched the program. The concept seemed to be that two teams of nerdy young men each build a robot. The robots are then placed into an arena where they attempt to destroy each other in front of a braying crowd of spotty teenage boys and *Star Trek* obsessives. All of this hosted by a smirking washed-up TV actor from an eighties sitcom set on a spaceship. One rickety-looking creation halfheartedly rammed the other with a pointy stick. The crowd went wild.

Outside the light had faded completely. I could feel the initial rush of the heroin starting. I knew it was happening because I found myself getting caught up in the TV show despite myself. I started admiring the skill and patience it would require to build such a robot. I began to wonder whatever happened to that sitcom from the eighties set on a spaceship. Did it get canceled? Surely not! Little eruptions of pleasure started in my spine, my chest, and my head.

I found myself wondering if everyone else was on heroin, secretly. Is this why they found TV like this so fascinating? Or was I defective, a faulty robot?

A robot was eventually declared the victor.

"Well, that was great," I heard myself saying. "Yeah." My roommate sighed, taking a sip from his lager. "Robots are brilliant."

I excused myself, flopped on the bed, and stretched out. Susan roused from her nod a little and muttered, "I feel so fucking good right now. . . ."

It did not seem possible to feel any better than I felt at this moment. Outside I could hear sirens, dogs barking, the comforting sounds of a metropolitan city. I was home at last.

7

MUSIC

I answered an ad in the *Melody Maker:*

GLAMOROUS ELECTRO-POP BAND seeks
KEYBOARDIST. Influences Duran Duran,
XTC, Japan, Chicks on Speed. Call.
Elektra.

The girl on the other end of the phone seemed
vaguely Eastern European. We arranged to meet
in a Camden bar. Having resumed my use of heroin I had initially intended to stop my attendance
of Narcotics Anonymous meetings. However,
one guy who was a regular at the Camden meeting, a grinning wide-boy ex–heroin addict turned
ticket tout named Michael had mentioned that
he had a council flat lying empty that he wanted
to sublet. He offered it to Susan and me on the
cheap. The temporary arrangement in Batman

Close was coming to an end, so I felt obligated to keep up the charade of twelve-step meetings in an attempt to secure the offer of the new place.

Also, now that I was attending meetings high on heroin, I found them a lot more bearable. Enjoyable even. I could take an active interest in other people's stories and sometimes even empathize with the poor fuckers. There was an initial twinge of embarrassment when I stood up to a roomful of applause, collecting a keychain celebrating ninety days sober while ripped to the gills on strong Afghan gear, but it soon subsided.

I started to get over my feelings of ridiculousness about "sharing" in group meetings. Loaded, I was expert at saying the right things: expressing the officially proscribed doubts and fears using the correct, crypto-therapeutic language. I learned not to roll my eyes or snigger when someone used an NA cliché around me. I was astounded by people's ability to use a cliché I had heard in recovery one million times before, as if they were expressing a truly original thought. Like this:

"You know what I realized I was doing?"
"What's that?"
"I was changing seats on *The Titanic*. You see?"

Or this:
"Listen. What you are feeling is fear. You know what *fear* means?"
"What?"
"Fuck Everything And Run. F.E.A.R. You see what I'm saying, mate?"

I met with Elektra and Paris from the band Liquid Sky in a little pub called the Good Mixer in Camden, right after my NA meeting in a nearby church hall. Right after the coffees and *amen*s I slipped into the bar and hammered back a couple of vodka tonics in quick succession. When I still played with the Catsuits, this bar had been the center of the indie rock scene in London. One could see some of the biggest faces in the Britpop scene rubbing shoulders with upstarts like us on a Friday night. Now it was populated by drunk Goth kids and tourists who showed up five years too late for the party. Somebody was playing Pulp's *Different Class* in its entirety. It was oddly like stepping back into 1997.

Two girls dressed like new-wave prostitutes staggered in on improbable heels. One of them wore a LIQUID SKY T-shirt strategically slashed across the tits and belly. This barely earned a sideways glance from the bar's jaded clientele. I looked up from my glass and waved over to them. They approached and the smaller of the two, a dark-haired girl with electric-blue eye shadow, offered her hand.

"Hi . . . I'm Elektra."

"Pleased to meet you."

The band was a three-piece: the diminutive Elektra on vocals, Paris on guitar, and a bass player who called himself Louis XIV. He was absent because he had to appear in court, having drunkenly crashed his Ford Cortina into a fence in Croydon. We talked and drank. My initial awkwardness faded away as the booze went down. Soon I was talking about the old days with the Catsuits and arguing over the merits of Suicide's later albums with them. They weren't nearly as pretentious as their personas and demeanors initially suggested. Elektra, the supposed renegade Russian heiress, was actually an Israeli girl with the less memorable birth name of Sue. Paris was actually a rather shy Dutch girl whose real name sounded like someone clearing their throat. We got on immediately. They remembered the Catsuits and there was a tense moment when they asked me what I'd been up to since the band split up. I shrugged.

"Oh, you know. This and that. Traveling . . ."

"Well, do you want the gig? If you're up for trying it out we're ready to start. You're the best person we've seen by miles."

This flattered my ego just enough.

"Cool. What were the others like?"

Elektra laughed. "A forty-year-old creep who kept telling me how sexy he thought Russian girls were, a butch lesbian who was really into Ani DiFranco, and a guy with a ponytail."

Rehearsals began immediately. They had written three songs that they gave me on a CD. On the back of their crude demo, the band had secured a prestigious slot doing a session for John Peel's show on Radio 1. The recording session was in a month and a half, and without a live keyboardist they could not perform any of the songs. I felt a familiar twinge of excitement. One of the first big things the Catsuits did was a session for Radio 1. Maybe somehow I could fluke my way back into the industry. I had the sense that somehow, I had stumbled upon a way out of the wilderness.

When I got back to Batman Close, Susan was nodded out in front of the little black-and-white TV, a cigarette burned down to her knuckles. I looked at her and closed the door behind me. I still had two problems: Susan and heroin. Susan roused from her stupor. In one movement I had my shirt off and was unlooping the belt from my jeans. I perched on the end of the bed, dumped some citric acid and heroin into the spoon, and began to cook up a hit.

"How did it go?" Susan slurred.

"Great. I'm in a band. We're called Liquid Sky."

"Thass . . . great."

"Yeah . . ."

I looked back at Susan, her slack jaw slumped onto her chest. Jesus, she looked bad. She was really giving up. I'd had a sense that maybe some of the spark would come back into her when she removed herself from the chaos of Los Angeles and found herself in a new city. But since we'd moved here, she barely ventured outdoors. I was the one who went out and found RJ, found the apartment, scored the heroin. Money was dwindling, one of us would soon need to get a job, and already Susan was whining about having no papers and how I'd have to be the breadwinner for the time being. She said it as if there was no one working without papers in London. The old girl seemed as if she were waiting around for death, but there was still something inside of me that wanted to hang around and find out what happened next.

Susan would have to go, right after I quit heroin again. I noted the irony of this thought, as I slid the needle into my flesh to hunt for a vein. But there was time. First and foremost, I had to do a good job with Liquid Sky and nail the John Peel session.

Then, I thought determinedly, feeding the shot into my arm, *then I can quit.*

8

MARCH

I am terrified. Vomiting. RJ has not answered his phone in days. I have been calling every ten minutes. Susan lies on the bed, twisting and turning in the duvet and cursing. I have taken to lying in the bathtub, fully clothed. Thank God our roommates are away for the weekend. It feels good to rest my head against the cool of the plastic tub and the tiles. At least for a moment. There is not enough money to risk going to Kings Cross to score. One rip-off and we would be fucked.

"Why the fuck do we have to rely on RJ!" Susan screams, on the verge of tears again. "You couldn't have found a fucking backup for emergencies?"

"Why the fuck is it always on me to do this shit?" I yell back, and that makes me cough and then the dry heaves start again.

———

"This is your fucking city! Your responsibility!"

"If you make me get out of this tub," I warn her, "I'm gonna throw you out the fucking window, do you hear me, cunt? I'll put you out of your fucking misery once and for ALL!"

She shuts up after that.

9

HABIT

It was depressing to realize that despite all of the promises to myself I had gotten a heroin habit again. I had not intended to get a habit. I mustn't have. But I had done the same fucking thing again: I had promised myself that I would use heroin only every other day to stop my body from building up a tolerance. But there was always an excuse for an exception to the rule. The weather was shite, there was nothing to do but sit around the place and get high. The weather was good, so why not have a little hit to celebrate? I was depressed, needed a shot to cheer me up. I was happy, needed a shot to enhance my happiness. The same old shit I had been pulling on myself since day one.

Every morning that I didn't wake up sick I'd think, *Well, I got a reprieve. No smack today, and I'm back on track.* In fact, being not sick and back on track would turn out to be a perfect excuse for a little hit. I'd think:

Did William Burroughs sit around, worrying about taking dope? Or did he just do it and then write immortal books?

Did Chet Baker worry like this? Or did he just get high and sing those beautiful songs?

Was Johnny Thunders a big crybaby pussy, skipping shots and worrying about getting a habit? Or did he just get on with it, and play his guitar like Jesus?

For Christ's sake, I'd tell myself, don't be such a fucking crybaby. And cook up a fucking shot already.

So, inevitably, the morning came that I woke up sick for the first time. My first thought was, Am I dope sick, or just sick? I couldn't tell. But I was wet. Soaked. I had sweat so much in the night that my side of the mattress was cold and soggy. And my stomach was feeling ominous. But the worst part was the beginning of the symptom that I knew meant withdrawal: the chills. Like my blood had been replaced by ice water. *Bollocks,* I thought, *you're dope sick. You fucking idiot.* My next thought was: *Well, you'd better get straight and figure out what's next.*

Susan woke up to find me perched on the end of the bed trying to shoot up. It was amazing that, having been off dope for almost three months, none of my veins seemed to have healed up. I'd imagined that I would be completely regenerated after three months of no needles, but it seemed like within days of starting to shoot up again my arms were mostly no-go areas. I was shooting into a vein in my foot, which hurt like a motherfucker. She blinked a few times and then muttered: "I feel sick. Fix me a shot."

"Fix your own fucking shot," I hissed. "I'm busy, you lazy bitch."

I had a rehearsal lined up for 4:00 P.M. I had to get hold of RJ and get enough heroin for the day. This was all happening at a very inconvenient time. Money was getting low, and we needed income. I made a vow to start looking for a job as soon as I copped some drugs. Miracle of miracles, RJ picked up first time. We agreed to meet in an hour.

I was waiting on a bench outside the tower block when he showed up, an hour late. I had been watching a bunch of young kids lurking outside a newsagent, grabbing smaller kids as they left and taking their loose change. I was feeling sick again. I handed him eighty quid and took four bags, hiding two of them in my pocket from Susan's probing eyes.

"You don't look well, mate," RJ said. "You all right?"

"Just a little sick. I should have saved a little for this morning, we've been bang at it recently."

———

"You got a doctor? I mean for juice or what-ever?"

"Juice?"

"Methadone. It's handy to have a prescription for days like this. There's a surgery in Shepherds Bush, I hear he's okay. You should get yourself on. It don't cost anything if you're out of work you know."

"I'm not ready to quit, RJ. I tried that once."

"Who says you have to quit? Doesn't do you any harm to have a little extra shit in case of emergen-cies. . . ."

After my experiences in the methadone clinics of LA, I was doubtful. But it was free. I thanked RJ and went upstairs to get Susan and myself well. Then I told her we were signing up for a doctor.

The surgery was deceptively normal, after my experience at the clinic on Hollywood Bou-levard. No crackheads asking for change. No heroin-addicted transvestites staggering around in hooker boots. Just a bunch of kids with runny noses and old folks with diabetes. We each filled out the required forms and waited around for an hour. Then we were called in together. Dr. Stein watched us impassively as we walked in and closed the door. He was a tall, cadaverous man whose hands and face seemed to be too large for the rest of his body. His expression was stony, and the room was silent except for the hum of the fluorescent lights. I felt like I was slipping into a confessional booth.

"How can I help you?" he asked eventually, after studying us for a while.

"Well . . . we wanted to ask about getting onto a methadone program."

"Hmm." Dr Stein started tapping at his computer, half-turned away from us.
"And you are both using?"

"Yes," we answered in unison.

"How much? Approximately."

"About a gram a day," I answered.

"Each?"

"Yes."

"That's a lot."

"Is it?"
"Yes, it is."

We weren't quite up to a gram a day yet, but it always helps to massage the figures. Dr. Stein tapped on the computer for a while and we both sat in silence. I glanced over at Susan, and she pulled a face. I mouthed *Asshole* to her. She nodded.

———

There were more questions. History of drug use, history of treatment attempts. It took a while. When you went through it all, piece by piece, I realized that I had been doing this longer than I had been playing music. I got a break at eighteen and played music professionally for two years. But I had been using heroin for the past four years solidly. It was a depressing statistic.

"Well," Dr. Stein said after collating all of the evidence, "I'm sorry to tell you that I can't help you right now. There simply aren't the places on the program at the moment. The best I can do is put you on a waiting list and get back to you."

Susan went into her crying, begging routine. She was really good at it. I had seen her do it to get drugs, money, and now she was using it to get on a methadone program. She started pleading and hot tears began to flood down her cheeks. He voice got higher, more insistent and demanding; she started to sob and her words became jagged and almost indecipherable.

"But . . . the money . . . we can't . . . and we're sick . . . and I'm starting a job . . . soon . . . and I'll lose it . . . if I can't show up . . . want to change . . . honest to God . . ."

It even took me by surprise. I put a stiff hand on her back and awkwardly said, "Hey, calm down. . . . We can manage, I suppose. . . ."

"HOW? HOW CAN WE FUCKING MANAGE? WHERE'S THE MONEY COMING

FROM? I CAN'T WORK SICK! WE'RE FUCKED!!!!!!"

Somehow, she prompted Dr. Stein onto the phone. He had a whispered conversation as Susan tried to control her breathing and stop sobbing. I knew it was going our way. I could pick out words here and there over Susan's sniffles and gasps for air: "very desperate . . . work lined up . . . I know he had one space available. Yes, they're married. . . ."

Dr. Stein hung up the phone.

"Okay, I managed to get you two on. Bear in mind that this is *highly* irregular. You're lucky that someone happened to drop out of the program this morning and I'm taking you both on as one case. You will have to take urine tests when you see me, and I don't tolerate any funny business. One dirty urine, and you're out of my program. And that counts for cocaine, too. Understood?"

"Yes, Dr. Stein," Susan sniffled. "And thank you."

We left the clinic with two prescriptions, written on special pink prescription pads. That means they were for narcotics. We each were given eighty milliliters of methadone linctus a day. Walking away from the clinic Susan laughed a little.

"I thought he was gonna crap his pants when I started bawling."

———

"Fuck, I thought *I* was too. That was pretty good."

"Yeah, well," she said somewhat bitterly, "I got a lot to cry about in my life. I just have to think about it for a while."

I looked at the prescription.
"Free fucking drugs," I laughed, "you can't get better than that. Maybe we could really get off dope using this."

"Oh yeah," Susan sneered, "You gonna join NA for real? Maybe we can practice our steps later."

"Fuck off."

"Then stop talking like a pussy. Quit dope! Jesus, sometimes I think you're going soft in the head."

10

JOBS (ONE)

Money is tight again. Money is always tight. The
interview is in a couple of hours. Roar of the
northern line and the shine of the shoes to Kent-
ish Town, nod nodding—mouth slack and wide—
a relaxed kind of autumnal mood. The leaves
are turning and covering the ground in yellows,
browns, and oranges, masking the dog shit and
the used condoms and the crushed cans of Tennent's. The city is almost beautiful.

His name was Brian Stoker. An old, overweight
man who huffed and puffed through his nasal pas-
sages as if it were a kind of tick or nervous habit—
like he was trying to dislodge some particularly
persistent mucus. The office of the magazine was
in his terraced house in a suburban North London street, and it seemed as if the place had not
been cleaned or redecorated in some years. The

carpets were brown and threadbare. The computers used to produce the magazine where cumbersome and outdated. There was a composite smell of mothballs, stale tobacco smoke, mildew, and ancient jizzum in crackling yellow Kleenex. I shook his hand, and he offered me a seat.

He regarded me silently for a while. I had made sure not to get too high before the interview so I could remain alert and enthusiastic about this new employment opportunity. Our money was low. We were facing the choice of heroin or rent this week, and I wasn't looking forward to being homeless again.

"Do you like country music?" he asked me eventually.

"Oh sure," I lied. "I like all types of music."
"I mean *real* country music. Not the shit that they're peddling in Nashville these days. The real stuff. Bluegrass. That kind of thing."

I started to warm up. I have an amazing ability to bullshit potential employers when my back is against the wall. My father went through a period of listening to old country. The Irish like country; they even have their own horrible "country" bands who play an unholy genre known as country and Irish—watered-down country standards mixed with Irish folk, usually performed by a perma-grinning fool in a tuxedo, wielding an accordion like an instrument of musical destruction. Suddenly my mind was able to pluck out a few of the names my father had mentioned.

———

"Oh sure, I know what you mean. I can't stand new country. The stuff I know is Hank Williams, Johnny Cash, and Charley Pride . . . those kinds of people."

"That's right!" my potential boss enthused, warming to me. "The new stuff is nothing but pop music! Real country couldn't get played on Nashville radio these days!"

"My father is a big country fan," I carried on, "so that's the music I listened to growing up."

Although not strictly a lie, this was a tremendous exaggeration. My father's country period lasted a year or two. At heart my father didn't really like music any more than he liked any of the arts. I recall him visiting a cinema once in my child-hood, a trip to see a matinee of *E.T.*, and even then he left halfway through to get a beer next door before returning for the credits. My father can proudly say he has never read any book apart from instruction manuals and how-to books. And music was just something to be on in the background when there was nothing to watch on TV.

Brian was asking me, "So you just got back from America, you say? What took you over there?"

"Work," I told him, the lies falling from my mouth effortlessly. "And an urge to travel. I worked at a music magazine in Los Angeles. It was a fun time, but I missed London. It was time to come back."

———

Brian got up, excited, and put a CD on. It was possibly the most excruciating music I had ever heard. It was a 1920s field recording of the "world-famous" yodeling cowboy Chip McGrits. I grinned and bobbed my head enthusiastically. Brian sat down and half-closed his eyes, dreamily listening to the crackly recording of the old dead bastard yodeling over fiddles and banjos. I was hit with the revelation that if funk was the logical conclusion to black music, then here was its white counterpart. After suffering through a couple of songs Brian informed me that I had the job and could start straight away.

I was employed for the first time in years, and it did not feel too great.

The hustle was this: Stoker produced a magazine that had various reprinted (without permission) articles from American country magazines and a few slim efforts penned by himself and some of his other wheezing, gray-haired friends in the London country scene. But the main body of the magazine was taken up with advertisements and reviews. It was my job to call people up and get them to advertise. I made a base salary, cash in hand, and a percentage of the advertising revenue.

Even for this kind of hustle it was despicably small-time. The only money the magazine made was in the reviews. Every day piles of CDs would arrive at the house for review in the magazine. The only people who bought the magazine were people who were reviewed in it. However, we would review anybody as long as they took out an advertisement in the magazine to peddle their wares. No advertisement, no review. The bigger the advertisement, the more enthusiastic the review. It was pathetic.

I spent most of my time in the bathroom shooting up. The lime-green tiles, the noise of Stoker's music, and my blood flooding into the barrel. Then, full of drugs and good feelings, I would swagger into the office and start hitting up people for money on the phone.

After two weeks I was moved out of the office and into Stoker's garage. He called it the "back office" but it was just a garage, a damp storage space piled high with unsold copies of the magazine in rotting brown cardboard boxes, a meager strip of carpeting, some electrical outlets, and a phone. I didn't mind so much. It was good to be away from the music.

I was obviously better at selling than most of Stoker's previous employees. I knew that I could make at least two sales a day—to keep him happy—and the rest of the time I could nod out in the back office, with the portable radio tuned to the BBC World Service. The voices of the reporters lulled me into very gentle space. Some of the people I called from Stoker's decade-old list screamed abuse when they heard my voice. One in particular started yelling hysterically when I said I was from *Traditional Country Music Monthly*.

———

"Stop calling here!" he yelled. "Every two weeks some new idiot calls me from your magazine asking me to advertise. I advertised once three years ago and it did nothing! I do not want to advertise with you again! Remove my name from your list, idiot!"

This guy's deal was accordions. He repaired them, sold them, reconditioned them. I didn't like his tone so I made a point of calling him at least twice a week and acting as if it were the first time I had ever called him, and I had no idea that he didn't want to be solicited anymore. Eventually a woman started answering the phone and I lost interest, as I couldn't provoke her into yelling abuse at me.

11

THE BBC

The John Peel session with Liquid Sky turned out to be the first thing we did as a band. Leading up to the show, I put in a lot of work. The band had recorded demos with producers but had only a rudimentary grasp of how to play their instruments. It was up to me to re-create the drums and keyboards on all of the tracks. Louis XIV had never learned to play the bass, and Elektra confided in me that they had removed all of his bass lines from the demos without his knowledge and replaced them with the work of a session guy. But they liked him and didn't want to hurt his feelings. We decided to program all of the bass lines in on the keyboards as well and to turn his bass low in the mix.

The first rehearsal took place at Elektra's house in Hoxton. She lived with a guy called Tom, who was also in a band. They were married, although Elektra insisted it was only to get her into the country. She told me that Tom was really into fucking transvestites and doing coke, two things that didn't really interest her. He worked a straight job in the city, doing phone sales, and then rehearsed with his band, the Ones, in the evening.

Tom disliked me immediately. Our first rehearsal I spent the whole day there with Elektra and Paris trying to make some sense out of the songs. It took us seven hours and a case of beer, but we finally got the rudiments of two tracks down. Paris plugged her fifty-quid replica Telecaster though Elektra's stereo and played along. Her guitar seemed to be constantly going out of tune. I stopped asking her to put it back in tune though, because she didn't seem entirely sure of how to do it and would take ten or twenty minutes to fiddle around with it. It would come back sounding exactly the same. The second time this happened, fearful of embarrassing her, I told her it sounded great and she smiled, relieved. Despite the fact that the guitars were out of tune and the bass player couldn't really play his instrument, I thought that the band had something. A certain ramshackle power. So I persevered.

Then, around five, Tom came home. He walked into the room silently and looked at us programming the synthesizer with obvious disdain.

"All right?" he grunted.

———

"Tom—this is our new keyboard player."

"Hi."

He listened to us for a little while. He quite obviously hated the music. We took a break, Elektra ran out to get more beers, and I tried to make conversation with him.

"Elektra tells me that you're in a band."

"Yeah. The Ones. You wanna hear our demo?"

"Sure."

He stuck a cassette in the stereo. Paris rolled her eyes at me and went to make a phone call. The music started. It sounded like fairly standard indie rock. And then the singing began. Before I said anything else, I asked Tom: "Are you the singer?"

"Yup."

Oh Jesus. It was terrible. It was one of the worst things I've ever heard. His voice had an almost uniquely tuneless and charmless sound to it. But I had to be polite. So I told him it was great.

"I know!" he said without missing a beat. "I can't believe it's you lot that got a Peel session first, to be honest. I mean, truth be told—Elektra's a great girl—but we piss all over your band."

I looked at him and he seemed completely serious.

———

"So," I asked eventually, "how's work?"

He then started telling me a long story about his job. He had to wear a suit, so he could sit on the phone and sell printing products all day. And whenever someone did a big sale, they had to go up and ring a gong that was in the center of the office, and everybody had to cheer. They kept a scoreboard up there, and at the end of the day the person with the lowest score had to take the wooden spoon.

"What's the wooden spoon?" I asked.

Tom looked at me like I was crazy.

"It's a spoon, man. It's made of wood. You know, a wooden spoon!"

"O . . . kay. What do you do with the wooden spoon?"

"Nothing! You have to keep it on your desk for all of the next day. And it stays there until you move up a place on the scoreboard."

"Oh. That's weird."

"Weird? It's fucking humiliating! I got the wooden spoon last week. I had to spend extra money on fucking coke just so I was aggressive enough to sell my way back out of the bottom. They're fucking assholes! A wooden spoon! Can you imagine?"

———

"Yeah. That's crazy. Why don't you quit?"

"Well, it's easy money. I couldn't afford to live in Hoxton if I didn't have a decent paying job. What do you do?"

"Well . . . at the moment I do sales for a folk music magazine. I work in some guy's garage. The magazine isn't real. It's just a hustle to get money coming in."

"That sounds depressing."

"It is, but I'm in that garage without any other people around me, and I can listen to the World Service. And they don't have gongs or wooden spoons, or some fool telling me I have to wear a suit so I can call people on the phone. But on the other hand, I am basically being paid five pounds an hour to sit in some crazy old bastard's garage in North London and harass people who repair accordions."

"That's absurd."

"I know. Life is absurd."

Bit by bit, over the next few weeks we got four songs ready for the Peel session. It was a weird time in British music. When I had left England, the whole Britpop thing had been falling apart. There was a very real sense that the party was somehow coming to a messy end. The new bands were all shit. The established bands like Oasis were well past their primes, and even the really great bands like Pulp had started going through midlife crises. In LA, nothing whatsoever was going on. As far as music goes, LA is something of a black hole. People there were talking about a glam metal revival. The handful of cool bands floated mostly below the radar. All of a sudden everybody sounded like either Matchbox Twenty or Limp Bizkit. By the time I found myself in London again, New York bands were all over the press. It started with the Strokes, and then the Strokes' imitators. Everything that bands had been doing in the UK suddenly seemed old. There was no effective response to the center of cool for the music universe suddenly being located on the East Coast of America. It seemed like everybody was looking for the next big thing in British music, so I figured, Why not us?

Our Peel session took place in a basement room at the Maida Vale studio. The place was huge and almost deserted. It had an eerie, hospital feel to it. The guys engineering the session had beards and wore cable-knit sweaters. They looked like a folk duo. We set up our equipment nervously.

"Okay, shall we do a quick run-through of one of the songs, to get levels?" the show's producer asked through the talk-back system.

I gave him the thumbs-up. I counted us in and we started to play.

Shit.

———

I had forgotten to tell them to turn the bass down. Everything sounded like a mess. It astounded me that we had a bass player in the band who did not know how to play bass, yet didn't seem to hear how terrible he sounded. He was completely unaware of his own incompetence. The song rattled along, and throughout it Louis's bass line bounced around, in the wrong key and the wrong time signature, like the noodlings of a mental incompetent engaged in some kind of music therapy, yet he stood there with a big stupid grin plastered on his face as if he were maybe Tina Weymouth or Bootsy Collins. We struggled on, and after the song ground to a halt I looked over to the window of the producer's booth. The engineers looked back at us in a kind of quiet puzzlement. I could see them thinking: "Is it meant to sound like this? Is this some kind of avant-garde thing? Or are they just completely inept?"

I cleared my throat and looked over to Elektra.

"Erm . . . I think some of the levels are a little off. Let me go over and speak to them."

I popped my head into the booth and called the producer over.

"Yes?"

"Erm . . . listen, is there any way you can kill the bass altogether? I mean, just take it out of the mix?"

———

"Well . . . sure. I can do that, but . . ."
"The bass lines are all programmed on the keyboards. We don't turn him up when we play."

"Oh."

He peered back through the window to look at
the band again. Louis was still standing there
grinning back at them.

"It's a kind of . . . care in the community thing," I
explained. "The girls just like having him around,
like Bez from the Happy Mondays. Except he
can't dance."
"I see."

I crept out and locked myself in the cavern-
ous bathroom. The bathrooms were clean and
smelled faintly of Pine-Sol. That was nice, at
least. Nothing worse than having to shoot up in a
dirty bathroom. I fixed and felt all of my anxieties
about the session melt out of my body, through
the soles of my feet and down into the tiles of the
toilet stall. It was time to go make history.

12

DECEMBER

On the Hammersmith and City line nodding—peaceful, all the way back to Kings Cross. It is Christmastime. I am waiting for RJ to show with the drugs—my breath hangs in the frosty air—and he appears from the blizzard like the monster in Shelley's *Frankenstein,* when the doctor chases his creation through the windswept landscape of Antarctica, and then I cut through to the toilet of the Kings Mall, where I fix with ice-cold, numb, and shaking hands, all the while, Frank Sinatra singing something festive like "The Little Drummer Boy" or "Silver Bells" is being piped into the filthy toilet.

And as the dope hits I know it is good shit—maybe a Christmas gift from RJ to me—and I fucked up my arm a little, and the black blood drips onto my shoes but I sit there—stupefied by

the heroin—as Frank's voice takes on a different tonality—spacing out dramatically—like the
record is *slooooowwwwiiinnggg dooooowwwww-*
-nnnnn, and the music sounds like it being piped
through a swimming pool filled with jelly.

On the train I think that maybe right here, right
now, I am the most beautiful man alive, because
everyone is beautiful when they are high: I start to
realize that the war on drugs is a war on beauty—a
war on perfection, because everything is perfect
on heroin—it is a war against the simple human
aspiration of complete contentment, and the
thought makes me sad—that we are waging such
a pointless and spiteful war against the noblest
part our own nature.

The train clatters into darkened tunnels, turning
the carriage black for a moment, and the thoughts
bubble and then fizzle—*Pop!*—like a thousand
Christmas lights burning out in unison—they
turn to stone and sink to the bottom of a

vast

inky

pool..

3

HELL IS OTHER PEOPLE

I soon found out that the move from Stoker's house to the garage had happened because Stoker had brought on a new staff member. She was from Newcastle; a thin pale girl who was supposedly there to lay out the magazine editorials. I had little to do with her. She seemed sad and a little beaten up. She smelled too, of thick heavy perfume seemingly to cover up for a lack of bathing. I recognized something in her and instinctively knew that she was an addict too. One day, after taking my mid-morning shot in the bathroom, I went to walk into the main office, stoned and forgetting about the move. Through the door I heard Stoker's hushed, wheezing voice:

"Do it ... like that ... keep going ..."

———

She gurgled, her mouth obviously full of the old man's cock, and I could hear a wet noise beating faster and faster.

"Right there . . . faster . . ."

I got the fuck away from there and listened to a report on the opium farmers of Afghanistan, passing out upright in my old office chair.

I owed the bank money. So every time Stoker cut me a check I had to bring it to a check-cashing place. I found one place on Fortress Road that would let me write checks to myself and cash them for 7 percent of the total. I had a book full of blank checks with a limit of a hundred pounds on them, so three, four times a week I would convert one into ninety-three pounds.

Temporarily at least our situation was fixed. I knew that the checks would run out one day soon and then I'd have to find another way to get by. But in the meantime there was money and long winter evenings and nothing but time. I caught up on reading. I ghosted around Soho at night when I was feeling rootless and energized. The neon lights bathed me and the dark strip clubs and doorways leading up to beaten old whores gave me a sense that I was among my own kind here. Occasionally I would score crack in the Soho alleyways from the black dealers ensconced in the shadows and hit the pipe in empty door-ways, while the sound of the city carried on all around me.

———

I'd sit there, looking out over the city I had left four years ago, a city I had once been a productive member of, and I would think that life could not get any more perfect, unless perhaps I was to wake up tomorrow and all that was left would be the night stretching from one end of the land till the other, and the neon would be on 24/7, and the city noise would be nothing but yells and raucous laughter and music blasting from bars and clubs.

After two weeks or so of being late to work because of picking up my methadone in Hackney I switched my methadone pickup to the Boots chemist in Tufnell Park, around the corner from Stoker's house. I did not like the new spot, despite its convenience for work. The old bitch that ran the joint would make me drink the methadone on-site. This was the rule for all new attendees. Despite the time I had under my belt at my old pharmacy, I was treated like I had wandered in off the street for the first time. There is no reasoning with pharmacists when the issue at hand is narcotics. In their eyes they are talking to you from a morally superior standpoint, so no words can be persuasive enough to make them relent.

At work one day, while I was doodling idly in my notebook, the new employee knocked and came in.

"Hi," she said.

"Hello."

"You busy?"

———

I shrugged and put the notebook down.

"Brian is out for a bit. I was bored." She smiled, perching on the desk.

"Oh yeah? There's nothing much happening in here."

"You're on stuff too, right?"

I eyed her suspiciously. "Stuff?"

"It's cool," she insisted. "I saw you at the chemist taking your dose. You didn't see me. I was buying tampons."

"Well," I said, at a loss for the right words. "That's nice."

"My boyfriend uses too. I mean, he's on a script too. He don't do the gear anymore. I made him stop. It was killing him."

Her name was Amy, it turned out. She seemed okay, a little slow, but okay. Two kids, a boyfriend out of work and on a script, and both of them hitting the crack pipe. She was working illegally—cash in hand—for Stoker to supplement their benefits. I didn't ask if the blow jobs were a part of the deal. I figured it would be best to keep my mouth shut.

Once she started talking it was hard to get her to stop. She had a crackhead's machine-gun mouth all right. She talked to me about anything, everything. That first day I stared off into space as she riffed on her kids, on her boyfriend, on reality television, on how bad Stoker smelled. I tried to listen to the World Service over her monologue, but found it was impossible to focus on anything else—her voice had a nightmarish quality about it, whiny and grating, and it seemed to reverberate from within your own head. Maybe that's why Stoker insisted that she put his penis in her mouth once a day.

I garnered all kinds of useless information about this woman. Where she lived (around the corner, across the road from the video store), what medication she and her boyfriend took regularly (Lustral—an antidepressant—and a blood-thinning medication for the boyfriend's deep vein thrombosis in his leg), her kids behavior ("Steve . . . come to think of it Steve and Jackie . . . They're both little shits"), and, her favorite topic, the fact that she had to drive to Kings Cross every night after work to score rocks.

"Why aren't there any decent crack dealers around here?" she would moan, repeatedly. "I hate having to drive all the way to the Cross to buy. I've never found a source for decent stuff around here. Why is that?"

"It's a mystery, I suppose," I would tell her.

The visits became more and more regular. I'm sure Stoker had the good sense to ignore her, but ever since Amy had discovered my "secret" I suppose she now thought of us as friends, and I became her unwilling confidant. She continually found excuses to come into the garage and bore me stupid with the minutiae of her life. After a week of this I started giving serious consideration to leaving the job.

I lasted another month. The job was easy, and the money was useful. But the main reason I had for liking the job—not having to deal with other people—was now irreconcilably ruined. One day after drinking my methadone in the chemist's I walked out onto the street and turned right instead of left. I went to McDonald's instead of Stoker's house and bought breakfast. Once I was half an hour late for work I left the restaurant and called RJ and set up a meet to buy some coke and heroin.

My time of being an employed citizen was, for now at least, over.

The kicker was that a month or so later I was watching the local news. The police raided the video shop right across from where Amy lived with her idiot boyfriend and her little shit children, after a tip off that people were selling crack cocaine out of there. What they found was a sophisticated operation where crack was on sale for bulk purchases. The bundles where stashed away in VHS copies of the latest movies. In the back room they were producing the rocks from powder cocaine in a mini production line. I laughed to myself, wondering if Amy had seen this yet.

Poor, dumb Amy.

14

NA

Jack was an eighteen-year-old kid with a shaved head that I thought at first was because of an affiliation to skinhead culture, but which I later discovered was because he was deeply ashamed of his natural, bright ginger locks. The first time I heard him speak was quite typical: it was during the Tuesday-night Narcotics Anonymous meeting in Camden. It took place in a filthy, cold room above a community center that everybody referred to as "the crack house." He shared a long, meandering story in which he came across as a rather buffoonish, comical character. In this story, some friends set him up on a blind date. As he was "sober" he had assumed his friends would be decent enough to set him up with a similarly sober girl. I remember at this point wondering if there was such a thing as a sober eighteen-year-old in London. It seemed entirely possible that

Jack was the only one—a kind of twelve-step Omega Man.

Anyway, the story continued. Of course the girl, Louise, was not sober. In fact, she showed up piss drunk to meet Jack. When he told her that he didn't drink or do drugs, she just smiled and said, "That's okay mate—all the more for me!"

I smiled. Nobody else did. What was it with fucking NA meetings? Nobody had a sense of humor.

The story continued and at one point featured a stone-cold sober Jack holding the girl's hair as she vomited twelve Bacardi Breezers and a döner kebab into the piss-stinking toilets of the Intrepid Fox on Wardour Street. The tale culminated on a night bus at two in the morning, with the obliterated Louise throwing strawberries (I can't remember where the strawberries came from) at the assorted drunks, psychos, hard men, and yardies riding the N87 to Wandsworth that night.

"What the fuck are you doing?" Jack whined, trying to grab her wrists before somebody beat the living shit out of him.

"I'm sharing the strawberries, dickhead!" came the reply.

I laughed. Everybody looked at me, Jack included. I held up my hands in a kind of *I'm sorry but it was funny!* way. He seemed genuinely aggrieved. I talked to him afterward, and that was when I realized that Jack wasn't even an addict. He was attending NA meetings because he thought he smoked too much weed. I shook my head sadly at him.

"You're eighteen," I said as gently as possible. "You're *meant* to smoke too much weed!"

I had offended Jack for the second time that night. He frowned and shot me an expression that only overly serious eighteen-year-olds can give.

"My addiction," he said, completely seriously, "Deserves as much respect as yours!"

So I filed Jack away mentally as just another asshole kid who needed to define himself through his problems—real or perceived. I thought it was cynical how the NA meetings embraced him, despite how obvious it was that he didn't have a problem. Now Jack was interacting with real-life addicts—crackheads, prostitutes, junkies—people he would never have had any contact with in the real world. For someone as guileless and naive as he seemed, this probably wouldn't be a good thing. Little did I know that in a matter of weeks I would be living with Jack, and everything would fall apart.

The meetings were now superfluous to my needs. I didn't have any friends in the program. But I did have some people I thought I could use to my advantage, and that kept me coming back.

Michael, the guy I knew from the Narcotics Anonymous meeting that I attended on Tuesday nights, still had the illegal sublet available on his old council flat in White Hart Lane. I asked around because I was informed that the lease was coming up on the flat share in Batman Close and we would all have to be out at the end of the month. The beer belly and the South African were going to take the opportunity to go backpacking. Susan and I were too high to make any adequate provisions for this event, so I decided it would be prudent to keep attending NA meetings to secure Michael's sublet. Susan stopped showing up with me, content instead to sit around the flat shooting heroin, watching daytime television, and smoking cigarettes.

But, of course, secrets do not last long in NA meetings and suddenly Jack was sniffing around Michael, wanting to get in on the action. One day Michael took Susan and I out to see his place. We took the tube to Seven Sisters, and then an aboveground train out to White Hart Lane. The area was run-down, nothing but high-rise council flats, shabby-looking semi-detached houses, low-end supermarkets, and corner shops. All they had out there was the football ground. To Michael, this was a selling point of Herculean proportions.

"You're just dahn the road from the ground, mate. It's fuckin' ace. You can hear 'em cheer whenever Tottenham score! Blinding!"

Michael obviously fancied himself as a wide boy. He looked like he would be handy with his fists. He was always in a Fila tracksuit and pristine trainers. He made his money as a ticket tout, now that he was out of the drug game.

"Fackin' Madonna's coming to play London soon! I 'ave five of us gonna get in the line for tickets. They'll 'ave a limit, but these fuckers are gonna go for a couple hundred each, mate! Nice little profit, yer know?"

The flat was on the seventeenth floor of a piss-stinking council rabbit warren. The elevator was literally sopping with urine and garbage. Susan made a disgusted face at me, but I just shrugged and told her to get in. Michael seemed entirely oblivious to it. He just seemed happily surprised that it was working. Inside, the place was a shambles. Dirty clothes lay all over the floor, and the air was stale. It had two bedrooms and a small bathroom. The main bedroom was at the back and had balconies where you could walk out and enjoy the view of the gray skies and the countless other high-rises. It was one of the most singularly depressing panoramas I have ever seen.

"I've not been back since I quit the brown, you know? I had to get out of here to get clean. Too many memories. Too hard to stay clean here, you know? I've been in this flat ten years, using for all of them. You see down there?"

Michael pointed to a muddy patch of grass, seventeen floors down.

"Yeah."

———

"A mate of mine jumped out my window and landed there. Broke both of his legs and his hips too. 'E's in a fuckin' chair now, the fuckin' cabbage."

"Why did he jump?"

"We was smoking rocks. I dunno. I s'pose he thought he heard something, you know what I mean?"

The deal was that the flat would be free in two weeks, and Susan and I could move in. The flat in Hammersmith had to be vacated in a week and a half. I asked Michael if there was any way he could clean out sooner than two weeks. He just shrugged and didn't answer.

"There's something else," he said. "I promised the other room to Jack. Do you mind?"

Michael saw the look on my face.
"'E's all right. He's just young is all. He won't be any trouble!"

Susan was livid, and we had an argument on the way home. She was already complaining about having to share the flat with Jack.

"You got a better idea, Susan? Maybe we should put a fucking down payment on our own place? I hear Chelsea's nice!"

"Fuck off. You should have told Michael no when he brought up Jack's name."

———

"You were there. Why didn't you tell him?"

"You're the man!"

"Yeah. That's why I've been out twice a fucking week praying with these cunts, picking up fucking key rings for making it nine months clean and fucking serene and having to listen to their fucking bullshit, and everybody asking me 'Oh, why don't you have a sponsor?' and all the rest of it! I've done my part. If this place ain't good enough, go get a fucking paper and start looking for another place yourself."

"Fuck that. Let's just call RJ."

"All right. That's more like it."

15

JOBS (TWO)

The regime under Dr. Stein was pretty good. I was back at my old pharmacy and once a day we went to Shepherds Bush Green to pick up our eighty-milliliter bottles of methadone. The methadone itself was luminous green and sickly sweet. Once the methadone kicked in I would be filled with good-natured cheer and get an insatiable appetite for sweets. At a bakery nearby, I would eat cream buns and custard tarts. I existed on a diet of methadone, Coca-Cola, chocolate bars, and pastries.

Over the next few months Susan and I met with Dr. Stein weekly. He would ask how we were doing. We would tell him that we were fine. Once in a while he would send one or both of us to the bathroom with a plastic bottle to take a urine test. While not actually curing the mental yearning to shoot heroin, the high doses of methadone we were being prescribed took away the physical need to do it. Without the relentless pressure of withdrawal gnawing at us we actually stopped doing heroin for a few months. However, once things were relatively stable for a while, I started to get bored. A junkie friend of mine used to remark how he would inject water whenever he didn't have heroin, and somehow it would make him feel better. Methadone did nothing for either the Pavlovian craving for the needle or for my need not to *feel*. Life was as ugly and as meaningless on methadone as on heroin, except now I didn't have my routine of scoring drugs and fixing to look forward to. I knew that there had to be a way to get around the urine tests, so I went to an Internet café and did a search on heroin's half-life in the bloodstream. It revealed that heroin tends to leave the system quite quickly, and you could give a clean urine test seventy-two hours after your last dose. So I resumed, regulating my use of heroin to the beginning of the week and weekends.

Once a week I attended the job center. Susan was ineligible for the dole, and I was eligible for only fifty-seven pounds a week. I was using at least a hundred pounds a week in heroin alone, so as unsavory as the prospect was I knew that I needed to find some kind of work again. After the experience with *Traditional Country Music Monthly,* I had vowed to stay away from regular employment. But, of course, cold hard reality intruded. In the job center, I sat across from an old woman with a pursed mouth who seemed to really resent her job. I told her of my work history: keyboardist in the Catsuits, then music video writing. It seemed so small and unimpressive when I tried to explain it to the woman.

"So . . . ," she monotoned, "would you be interested in doing something with music again?"

"Oh yeah. Do you have something?"

She tapped into her computer for a moment. She said, "Here we go," and half-turned the monitor toward me. On screen it said: "VIRGIN MEGA-STORE, OXFORD STREET. SALES ASSIS-TANTS RQD (IMMEDIATE)."

"I'll set you up an interview, then, shall I?"

Well, Jesus. I was desperate. The night before I had flicked on the television and saw none other than my old band mate, Laura, presenting a TV show on Channel 5. She looked exactly the same. I sat watching her, with a snoring junkie wife on the bed next to me. I had less than a hundred pounds in the bank and was shooting up into my legs. I didn't look exactly the same. I looked like the portrait in the fucking attic. Part of me wanted to stand up and tell the old whore to fuck off, that I'd eat dog shit before I'd work in a Virgin Megastore, but I fought the urge. I needed something straight away, or there'd be no more drugs.

"Yes," I said quietly. "Set up the interview."

My first day on the job I wandered around the shop floor in an ill-fitting T-shirt, trying to avoid talking to people until my lunch break. I was working five days a week, my schedule changing every week. Once a month I'd have a weekend off. I was paid seven pounds an hour to restock the shelves and work the tills. It was mind-numbingly boring work, made worse by the giant video screens that looked down upon us everywhere we went, blaring out terrible songs every fifteen minutes. That was the gimmick—every fifteen minutes there would be a great sound like the whole shop was about to take off. And then these huge video screens would flicker into life and a song would come on. The second or third time this happened I realized that it was the same fucking song. The same video. I found myself inadvertently singing along. Oh Jesus, I thought.

I walked over to the supervisor, a large Jamaican girl who seemed ruthlessly efficient and far too dedicated to a job that was the non-food equivalent to working in a McDonald's. Her name was Jenna.

"Jenna," I yelled over the music, "are they gonna play the same song all day long?"

"Huh?"

"On the big screen. They've played the same song three times already!"

"Oh yeah. The record company buys the screen for a block of time. Usually a month or so."

"A month! I'm gonna be hearing this shit for a month?"

———

"Oh, don't worry. After a while you stop noticing it. I didn't even realize it was on."

After two weeks I was ready to lose my mind. On my early shifts I'd be in there at 8:30 A.M. to endure a start-of-day pep talk from one of the managers. Usually some meaningless nonsense about how well the store was doing, what a great guy Richard Branson was, and how to watch out for shoplifters. Then, even before the store was open to the public, I'd hear the sound.

WHUUUUUUUUUURRRRRRRGHHHH-
HHH.

That was the sound of the screens fading into life. The song started with a drum intro that turned my blood cold. I couldn't block it out. I tried everything. I brought drugs to work and got high in the bathroom. I even walked around with earplugs in, but when I walked right past Jenna, ears plugged and oblivious one day as she called for me, I got busted, receiving an official reprimand. So no more earplugs. Sometimes I would wake up in the middle of the night with that same fucking drumbeat playing in my head. I felt like I was being subjected to some intricate form of psychological terrorization.

And the customers. Jesus. If you made the mistake of making eye contact with any of them then you'd be stuck for an hour.

———

"Excuse me, where would I find Mariah Carey's new album?"

"Excuse me, do you have a bossa nova section?"

"Excuse me, are things filed by first name or surname?"

I learned to perfect the art of walking purposefully with a bunch of random CDs in my hand. If anybody stopped me to ask anything I'd tell them, "I'm terribly sorry, I'm assisting another customer at the moment. Somebody else will be happy to help you" before cutting out. The building was so big that I could pass entire days going from one floor to the next, picking up a CD from the storeroom, carrying it to the next floor, taking a break, walking through the jazz section flicking through CDs. Anything but doing actual work. And, of course, stealing.

Everybody stole. But nobody stole as ruthlessly and efficiently as I did. The process was simple. Staff got searched when leaving for the day, but not on lunch breaks. Wandering around the West End on a break, I stumbled upon a Japanese language college. I entered and located an empty locker on the third floor. Sensing an opportunity, I bought a padlock and fitted it. Then on lunch breaks I would make the journey with my jeans stuffed full of stolen CDs and store them in the locker for collection at the end of the day. I wasn't the only one stealing, but I was the only one with such a well-thought-out system. I took home approximately twenty to twenty-five CDs a day. Sometimes RJ would take CDs in exchange for heroin, and I started stealing to order. For the three months that I worked there, up until the time they let me go rather than renew my contract, I had all of the heroin I wanted. I was a king, I suppose. But unbeknownst to me, this rare moment of serenity would be fleeting. Life was about to take another turn.

16

THE FUCKUP

The living arrangement with Jack was the beginning of the end in many ways. The first problem was the fact that I moved out of Dr. Stein's catchment area. A catchment area is the area immediately surrounding a doctor's surgery. Dr. Stein had drilled into both Susan and I the importance of telling him if we moved, as he could legally prescribe methadone to us only so long as we remained in his area. Of course, the move from White City all the way north to Tottenham was bound to cause us big problems. So we simply never mentioned it. After all, what he didn't know couldn't hurt him, right?

The hammer started to fall three weeks after moving in with Jack. Susan and I slept on mattresses in the large bedroom at the back. Despite taking two weeks to prepare the flat, all that

Michael had managed to do was put his clothes into messy piles and stick them in the corner of the room. Jack was ensconced in the smaller bedroom down the hall.

Now keeping our methadone prescriptions under wraps from the others in NA was even harder. Jack suddenly decided that we should all be friends since we were living in the same place, and he kept inviting us out to pubs and clubs with him. I went once. I thought that when Jack invited me to a club, that surely all bets must have been off in regards to his supposed sobriety. After all, what on earth would one do in a nightclub in Brixton without even a few beers?

The answer came soon enough. One would stand around, sipping tonic water or Coca-Cola, watching everybody else have a good time, listening to jungle music, stone-cold sober. Jack was immediately on the floor dancing, leaving me to watch him in increasing disbelief. I started to wonder if in fact Jack was not some kind of mental subnormal.

The day that everything fell apart started off like any other. Susan and I had our weekly meeting with Dr. Stein at the surgery in Shepherds Bush. I was already wondering about the possibility of finding somewhere else to live. Living with a genuine NA'er was tiring, especially as Susan and I were now both expected to attend meetings with Jack. We would have to come up with continuous cover stories to avoid getting roped into attending three meetings per week. I could sense that

Jack was getting suspicious. When I gave in and went to a meeting with him one day, he told me as much. We were hanging around in a nearby McDonald's waiting for the meeting to start and he said, "I'm worried about you."

"Why?" I laughed, trying to sound casual but knowing what was coming.

"You barely attend meetings anymore. You never share when you do. You've been coming around for ages and you still don't have a sponsor. I know that you two are clean, but, you know, my sponsor, David, says that sobriety isn't enough!"

"Oh yeah? It's enough for me. What else am I supposed to do? Do a fuckin' song and dance?"

"He says that people like you are . . . what did he say now? Yeah—*dry drunks*. You're not drinking, but you're still exhibiting all the symptoms of being sick."

"Jack," I said patiently, "for one, I'm not a fucking drunk. I never have been. Two, I don't know David and David doesn't know me—or Susan—so really his opinion is of no interest to me. If coming to meetings as often as I feel I need to and staying off drugs isn't enough, then, you know, fuck it. Maybe I shouldn't come. Why don't you go to meetings with David, since you find him so utterly fucking fascinating?"

Jack backed off, startled a little by my outburst.

———

"Wait! Look, of course staying clean is what's important. It's just . . . I don't want to see you . . . go back on it, right?"

"You don't know nothing about it," I snapped. "You've never done gear. You don't know what it's like. You can't fucking judge me! Anyway, it's time for our precious fucking meeting, okay?"

"Shit. Okay, man. Chill the fuck out."

So I knew that this situation couldn't carry on indefinitely. I was pondering this as the nurse called Susan and me into Dr. Stein's office. Walking in and closing the door behind us, I noticed that Stein looked even more glum-faced than usual.

"Sit down."

We did.

Saying nothing, Stein took out the pink prescription pads that they use for narcotics and scribbled down our weekly prescription. This was unusual. He usually asked a bunch of questions, asked for a piss test, something. But today there was nothing, just Stein writing, stonily silent, pressing down so hard that I thought his pen might tear a whole through the paper.

"There you go," he said, tossing the prescriptions at us, "your final prescriptions. Now don't come back, either of you."

_____

Susan and I just sat there in silence. Stein glared at us. I started racking my brain. I knew that I couldn't have given dirty urine the last time. I hadn't used heroin in a while. Since getting the heave-ho from Virgin, heroin was temporarily a luxury item.

"I don't understand," Susan began.

"Where do you live?"

"One-oh-nine Batman Close—" I began.

"*Bullshit!* I sent you a standard letter, because your last urine test proved inconclusive. It wasn't positive, probably some over-the-counter medication you have been taking, but it was enough to render the test inconclusive. I sent you a standard letter to inform you of this, as the rules dictate. The letter was returned to me with the notice that you *no longer live* at that address."

"Look, Dr. Stein," I stammered, in full damage control mode, "I was going to tell you! The lease came up on the flat and we had to vacate. We're somewhere temporary—only for a few weeks, and we're looking for a new place right in the area. That's why we didn't tell you!"

"Oh yes, I'm sure. You people are always so fucking innocent! You probably have four or five doctors prescribing to you, right? You don't give a shit whether I lose my license! I've been nothing but good to the pair of you!"

———

I was stunned. Dr. Stein was genuinely hurt by our deception. Although, I must admit, when he mentioned his suspicion that we had more than one doctor prescribing methadone to us, my first thought was: *That's possible? I gotta try that.*

Susan chimed in. "Dr. Stein, it's true! We didn't want to fuck up our prescriptions, that's all! We're only out of White City for a month, tops, until we can find a local flat again! We're sleeping on a friend's floor at the moment. Please . . . please, don't kick us out. Things have been going really well recently! We're getting it together. . . . Oh Jesus . . . please don't kick us out. . . . It's not fair!"

Susan was about to go into her crying and wailing routine again. Stein cut her off with a wave of his hand.

"It's too late. The wheels have been set in motion. You must give me your new address, and another doctor has to take over your care. It's expressly prohibited for me to prescribe to patients outside of my catchment area. I'm sorry, but I can't help you anymore."

We returned to Tottenham in silence. We drank our methadone from the bottles on the train ride home. Everything was wrong. Ascending in the pissy elevator to the seventeenth floor of our block of flats, the situation was about to deteriorate further. There were people in the flat. Usually Jack would fuck off during the daytime, but he was here and so was Michael. The cunts were both sitting around in our bedroom.

———

I opened the door and saw them, huddled in conversation.

"Oi!" I yelled at the pair of them, "What you doing on our room?"

Michael looked up. He just said: "Can you come in here a minute?"

Susan and I walked in silence toward them. Michael and Jack were sitting on the only two chairs in the room. Michael pointed toward the mattresses and said, "Sit down." We did. Michael and even dumb, eighteen-year-old Jack were now towering over us. I started to feel anger rise in my chest. Susan kept her mouth shut and looked at the floor.

"Fucking problem?" I asked.

"I think so," said Michael, "Jack here . . . and me too actually . . . we're worried that you aren't really a part of the program anymore. I mean, I know that you sometimes show up to the odd meeting, but . . . well, it's been a long time you've been coming around. A long time. Neither of you have a sponsor, which to me . . . well, I just don't get it."

"What don't you get?" I demanded. "I don't want a sponsor. When I bump into someone at one of these meetings who I think will have the first clue about where I'm coming from, then sure, then I'll have a sponsor. Until then, I'll do it myself."

——

"That's not the way the program works!" Jack laughed.

"Don't tell me about the fucking program, Jack. I went to my first meeting five years ago in LA, remember? You were thirteen fucking years old Jack. I'm not listening to any fucking lectures from you, mate. I show up. That's where I'm at right now."

"Anyway," Susan interjected, "how is any of this your business? What, you sublet a flat to us and suddenly you're monitoring our recovery? Where do you get off, Michael?"

"Look, love," Michael shot back, "for all intents and purposes, I'm your fucking landlord, okay? And there's some shit I can't tolerate in my flat these days."

"Oh, so we can't live here unless we start showing up to more meetings and being good little patients? So you're the king of recovery now? What? If I don't get a sponsor are you going to revoke my ex-junkie license?"

He ignored me. He looked at his hands for a long time. Then he looked up.

Michael said: "You're still using. The pair of you."

"Bullshit," I hissed. "I might not buy into all of this fucking twelve-step stuff, but you can't just accuse us of . . ."

——

Jack had his moment of triumph. He reached down to the floor and picked up the evidence. One of my empty, brown medicine bottles labeled "Methadone linctus. 80 mls."

"You wanna tell me just what the fuck you were doing snooping around in my fucking room, cunt?" I spat.

"Fuck off! I was looking for that book you borrowed off me!"

Ah, the book. About a week before Jack had been telling me about a book he had just read, *A Sense of Freedom* by Jimmy Boyle. Apparently he was Scotland's most dangerous prisoner, and then he became a sculptor. It sounded quite mindless, but I had made the mistake of feigning interest. Jack had insisted that I borrow it. I declined. "But I'm done with it! You can hang on to it for as long as you'd like." For a quiet life I had taken the tattered paperback, put it on the desk in my room, and promptly forgotten all about it.

I sat there, quiet for a moment. I didn't like sitting in front of the pair of them like a naughty schoolboy anymore. I stood up, so I was now looking down on them.

"Look. I relapsed. I'm a junkie. Michael, you know what I'm talking about . . ."

Jack went to chip in, but I dismissed him with my hand.

———

"Listen, between you and me, Michael, the boy wonder here doesn't have a clue what he's talking about. You know this. He's a moron! *You* know. How many times did you fuck up before you got clean this time? And how long has it been, huh? Less than a year, right? So you don't know what's around the corner any more than I did. I fucked up! I got a habit again. I got on a methadone program. Are you seriously telling me that you are shocked that a fucking heroin addict relapsed? Is this news to you?"

"You lied to me. You lied to the fellowship. You stood up there and took key chains for being clean for thirty days, sixty days, six months—"

"Who did I hurt, Michael?"

"You led us on! You *lied*."

"And you've never lied when you've been using?"

"But he isn't using now!" Jack piped up.

"Shut up, cunt!" I screamed at him. He kept his ass on the chair. I looked back to Michael.

"So what are you saying?"

"I want you both out of here."

"You fucking serious?"

"Yeah."

———

I ran my fingers through my hair. I looked down at Susan. We had separately, and together, been evicted so many times, from apartments, from motel rooms, from other people's homes, that she just shrugged and looked at me as if to say "c'est la vie."

"Fine. We'll be out by the end of the week."

"I want you out tonight."

"No way."

Now it was Michael's turn to stand. He had a few inches on me, and meat on his bones.

"I want you both out tonight."

"I just paid you rent for the week."

"You'll get it back."

"Now?"

"Not now. When I have it. Now fuck off. If you don't wanna leave, I'll come back with some mates and I'll chuck you out. You know that I ain't fucking around, right?"

I knew. I looked down at Susan. "Pack our shit up," I told her. "I'm gonna go find us a place."
I left her there with Michael and Jack. I didn't want her coming with me. I didn't need to hear her fucking voice on top of the chatter in my own

head. I cursed and punched the elevator doors as it brought me down to the ground floor. Outside the rain was pissing down. The gutters were filling up with filthy water, and I was racking my brain about where to go. I remembered the hooker motels around Kings Cross and decided to hit there. Any motels that rent rooms by the hour had to be cheap.

On my way out of the flat, Michael had the audacity to yell after me: "Don't give up on sobriety, mate. When you're ready to come back, the meetings will be there for you."

I paused by the door, and gave him my considered response.

"You can suck my dick, Michael, you fucking faggot."

I slammed the door, made my way down to the rain-blasted streets. I felt strangely liberated. This is when I functioned at my best, with my back completely up against the wall. I knew that the situation at the bank wasn't good. We had maybe a hundred pounds to our name. The rain kept coming down on me, oblivious to my situation.

17

DOWN AND OUT
ON MURDER MILE

We stayed in Kings Cross for two sleepless nights. The first night that we were there I woke up in the early hours, covered in bites from the bugs that lived in the mattress. The motel was a run-down shithole off Caledonian Road, and the room was in the basement floor and didn't even provide sunlight. I called Dr. Stein's office and informed them that we were now homeless and looking for a place to live. His nurse warned me that unless we found something by our next scheduled visit, our prescriptions would be canceled. I hit the papers looking for a place.

Susan got on the phone to her father in LA and pleaded for money. Over the years she had burned both of her parents down for money, but surprisingly the old man came through for her this time, wiring two thousand dollars by Western Union. When I expressed surprise she just laughed.

"They're just happy that I'm not in LA anymore. That has to be worth a couple of thousand, right?"

I looked at her and silently wondered just who had gotten the best out of that deal.

I found a flat that lay above a shoe repair place on "Murder Mile"—Upper Clapton Road. We saw the place at ten in the morning and took it straight away. It was a pit, but we couldn't afford to waste money in the motel any longer. The landlady's son showed us around, and something about him gave me the impression that after we said we wanted the flat that he might try and sell us a stolen cell phone or some bootleg DVDs. I figured the uglier and more fucked-up the flat was, the less chance that they would be interested in what went on behind closed doors. Total ano-nymity was my goal, and I got it.

The first night that we were there, I turned on the TV and a local news reporter was standing out-side of our front door.

"They call it Murder Mile," he said, looking straight at the camera, "a section of East London that has more shootings per capita than any-where else in the UK. Today, Homerton Hospital announced that they were hiring doctors from South Africa—doctors more adept at treating

gunshot wounds—to deal with the spiraling con-
sequences of Murder Mile's crack-fueled explosion of violence. . . ."

The landlady was an ancient Indian matriarch
who asked no questions as long as the rent was
paid roughly on time. She sat behind the counter
of the shop downstairs like a wooden statue—
unblinking and unmoving—with the smell of
leather, shoe polish, and glue heavy in the air like
a kind of incense. She said nothing when I slipped
the three hundred pounds cash over the counter to her, just gave a slight nod of the head. She
was draped in yellow-gold jewelry and her entire
being seemed to shimmer in the dull light.

The steel door next to the shop led to a concrete
hallway with a blinking yellow light illuminating
it. Then up the brown-carpeted twisting staircase
to the third floor. The room itself was shabby,
cold, and small. The carpet was dark brown and
threadbare. Our tiny, portable black-and-white
television sat upon a rickety chest of drawers in
front of the dirty, collapsing bed. There was a
small, unused kitchen and a dark, bloody bathroom.

Sometimes you could hear mice in the walls, in
the quiet hours before dawn. We started using
heroin in earnest again. I watched Susan shrink
and age here, dramatically—she lay on the bed
mostly whining about dope sickness and fixing
drugs and stinking the place up with the stench
of the living dead, but sometimes, when I was
too sick to move, she would relent and make the

convoluted journey from Murder Mile to Hammersmith to pick up our drugs from RJ. But I soon realized that waiting for her to come back was worse in a way than making the journey myself. The terrible sense of stasis, of time standing still, slipping backward even, while bad daytime television crackled out of the set and the demons and the sickness flayed me alive in the bed was more unbearable than making the journey myself—sweating and shaking in packed commuter trains and watching the stations grinding by.

At least then the countdown—Latimer Road . . . Shepherds Bush . . . Goldhawk Road—gave the sense of a building climax. And then in the toilet of the Kings Mall, a depressing Stalinist concrete façade, holed up in the filthy dark cubicle with one foot wedged against the lockless door listening to the homeless guy in the next stall take a spluttering liquid shit, the smell filling the whole place, I'd cook up my shot and thread the needle into my gooseflesh, probing for a vein . . . thick black blood dripping down my forearm, spotting my jeans, forming in dark pools on the piss-wet tiles.

Once the shot was in my bloodstream the homeless guy's shit started to smell like a home-cooked meal and I would feel pure pleasure in my guts instead of fear and hunger, and the long ride home became a reverie—relaxed and languid—handsome and perfect on the Hammersmith and City Line to Kings Cross, nodding in time to the train's slow-motion lurches.

———

Susan's face was a constant reminder of my condition. I looked at her with the same terrified fascination with which a drowning man might look upon a sack of bricks that had suddenly appeared chained around his neck. Without even a cunt that I wanted to penetrate she was an obsolete commodity, ossified into clichés by her constant self-pitying.

Once we moved into the flat on Murder Mile, Dr. Stein was able to palm us off onto another methadone clinic—Homerton Drug Dependency Unit, where we found ourselves under the care of Dr. Ira. Stein handed us our last prescriptions and a sealed letter with our case histories to give to our new jailer.

In Dr. Stein's clinic I had little to no interaction with other addicts. The waiting room was full of people with common or garden ailments—old ladies with varicose veins, pregnant women, ugly runny-nosed children. The junkies tended to recognize one another, but they rarely interacted. Walking into the doors of Homerton for the first time, I realized things would be very different. Junkies were everywhere. As I was walking in one was arguing with a sour-faced, gray-haired old lady behind the reception desk about something or other. He looked cadaverous and vengeful; he spat curses at the old woman, who looked at him like he was a hideously animated piece of feces.

"If you don't sit down and stop talking," the old lady said, "I'm going to call security."

———

"Call 'em ya fucking cunt! I dare yer!"

She picked up the phone. She dialed a number and said, "Security?"

The guy punched the desk. "Fuck you!" he screamed at her. "I'm fucking going. Tell that Jew-fuck Ira to stick his fucking mefadone up his arse! Fuck this shit! I ain't coming back! Twats!"

He stormed out of the glass doors and into the parking lot. There were four or five others sitting around in the waiting room, silent in their misery. I walked over to the old woman behind the desk, gave her my name, and was told to wait. After a few minutes, Susan and I were called into an office to meet Dr. Ira.

He gestured for us to sit down on the two plastic chairs by his desk. I handed over the envelope and Ira studied the paperwork on us both. He left us sitting there like that for a good five minutes. I could hear him breathing in the quiet little office. I could hear Susan's bones creaking as she shifted position on her seat. Eventually I began: "Dr. Ira, if you have any questions about—"

He shook his head and carried on reading. He was taking an extraordinarily long time to read a single sheet of paper. Eventually he put the paper down and peered over at us.

"The first order of business," he said, "is to come up with a treatment plan for the two of you. A time frame, if you will."

———

"Okay," I said. "A time frame for what though?"

"For detoxification."

I let this information sink in. Then, remembering something Dr. Stein had said to me during one of our sessions, I said: "But our last doctor recommended that we stay on methadone for the foreseeable future. He said that the longer someone is on methadone, the better the chances of them staying off heroin when they do detox."

"Poppycock!" Dr. Ira laughed. "Dr. Stein sounds like a typical softly-softly man. That kind of attitude never helped anybody to get off drugs! It's best not to pussyfoot around with these things, get it over with as soon as possible. Rather like ripping off a plaster, yes?"

Dr. Ira started writing in his file.

"Excuse me."
He stopped, sighed, and closed his file. He took off his glasses, rubbed his eyes dejectedly, replaced the glasses, and looked at me in exasperation. "Yes?"

"Well, I don't think that I want to detox. I'd like to remain on methadone for a while. This is the best my life has been in . . . five years at least. I don't think I'm ready."

"Well." He smiled. "You'd better be. Because we do have a problem here on two fronts. One is that

I—and my hospital—do not believe in long-term methadone maintenance. We see it as counter-productive. In layman's terms, our position on providing opiates to opiate addicts is that it is rather like providing cars to joyriders. You are not solving the problem, but rather rewarding the negative behavior. But the other problem is one that is much more pressing, for both of you."

"What is that?" Susan asked.

"Well, I see here that Dr. Stein was something of a liberal prescriber. Eighty milliliters of metha-done daily, hmm? I'm afraid that that just won't do. The most you will get here is fifty milliliters, so in a way you will be starting a detox of a kind . . . right now."

"But—" I started.

"This is not something I can discuss with you. We have a cap here of fifty milliliters. Eighty millili-ters is absolutely out of the question."

"Then I want to be treated somewhere else."

"Do you have the money to see a private doctor?"

"No."

"Well, unless you're willing to move into another catchment area, I am afraid I am all that you've got. Don't worry, we'll make you nice and com-fortable."

———

Susan and I just looked at each other in shocked silence. Dr. Ira scribbled a note on a piece of paper and handed it to us. It wasn't the regular pink prescription slip we had been receiving from Dr. Stein.

"What's this?" I asked.

"It's a prescription notice for seventy milliliters of linctus that will be reduced by ten milliliters a week until you are at an acceptable dose of fifty milliliters. You go into the back office and you will be given a card. Each day you present yourself to this clinic, your card will be stamped, and methadone will be dispensed."

"To take home?"

"Of course not. You drink the methadone on-site."

Immediately I felt myself tensing up. The first week or so that I had been on methadone, I had taken my dose first thing in the morning. I found that by six or seven in the evening I was in a mild state of withdrawal. After a few restless nights' sleep I worked out that it helped to take forty millitliters first thing in the morning and forty milliliters at night before bed. Not only was the bastard forcing me to reduce my dose, now he was telling me how to take it. I explained to the doctor about my routine for taking the medication. He just smiled at me, the patient look of a man trying to explain—again—that the rules had changed and that I had no say in what happened next.

———

"You take your dose on-site. Take-home doses are a privilege to be earned. If you don't like how my hospital is treating you, the door is not locked. You are free to leave treatment at any time."

After drinking our allotted dose in a windowless back room overseen by an officious woman wearing glasses, we split, cursing the place.

Walking out into the hospital parking lot, Susan and I were approached by a tall figure with a mop of unruly black hair and skin pressed tight against prominent cheekbones. Susan was lighting up a cigarette and the figure said, "Spare a fag?"

Susan nodded, handed him one, and lit it for him.

"You two under Dr. Ira?"
I nodded, "You?"

"Nah. Fuck that. I don't do that shit. Once those fucking methadone clinics get their claws into you"—he motioned to his wrist as if locking the key on a set of handcuffs—"especially that cunt. My ex-missus used to see him. She used to come home in tears every fuckin' Wednesday. A right bastard."

"Yeah, he's reducing us already. He wants us down to fifty in a fortnight."

"Yeah. Says he won't prescribe over fifty, right? I know. Heard it all. You know that there's no limit to what they can prescribe legally? Mate of mine is on two hundred milliliters a day. Has been for years. That fifty milliliters rule is just something Ira thought up. But look, if you ever need extra..."

He reached into his pocket and brought out a handful of glass ampoules.

"What are they?" I asked. Susan leered at the ampoules.

"Methadone amps. Mate of mine gets 'em from a private doctor in the city. Trades 'em to me. You can shoot these and it won't dirty up your urine test."

We had started walking back toward the street together.

"I'm Steve Cook, by the way."

We shook hands.

"Do they feel good?" asked Susan. "The methadone amps?"

"Yeah! They're good. Not as good as the real thing but as least you get a hit from it, unlike the fucking juice. Stick some Ritalin in there and it feels like a speedball, though."

"You got any Ritalin?"

"That's where I'm going now. Kid I know has ADD. But 'e doesn't react well to the Ritalin. His mum sells 'em to me."

———

Steve gestured to a block of council flats overlooking the hospital.

"How much?"

"Three quid each."

"D'you mind if we come up?"

Steve laughed, "More the merrier, mate. Eh—you ain't old bill are you?"
We had a laugh about that as we went up to score the pills.

Steve rapped on the door, and a heavy, tired-looking woman answered it. She was sucking on a cigarette. "A'right Steve," she said, beckoning him inside. Susan and I stood about on the balcony, looking at the rows of identical front doors.

"You think he's on the level?" Susan asked.

I shrugged. I hoped so. It had been a long time since I had done anything approximating a speedball. I hadn't injected coke since leaving LA, for fear of getting into the kind of mess that I had back in the States with a coke habit. But after today, after listening to that red-nosed bastard doctor lay down the law about how much methadone I should take a day, and where I would be taking my methadone, I was in the right headspace to get good and fucked up.

18

JULY

I am scoring crack in Kings Cross. It is my twenty-fourth birthday. I am playing a show tonight with Liquid Sky in Tufnell Park and I am nervous. Louis, the incompetent bastard, promised to score some cocaine for me, and of course it fell through at the last minute. He seemed utterly bemused by how pissed off I was. We have two hours following sound check before we play the show. I decide to go to the Cross and risk the street dealers in the hope of getting some rocks.

Wandering the street making eye contact with the various dodgy-looking people loitering by the station, I find a runner who immediately tries to bully me into buying from him. "My guy is in the motel there," he says, nodding to one of the many horror motels that dot this neighborhood, "Gimmie the cash and I'll come back with the stuff."

"I'm not a fucking tourist. I'm not buying unless I can try some first."

"Nah, too many cops."

He smiles at me, his gold teeth glinting with a vague kind of threat.

"Just gimmie the cash," he says as if talking to a remedial student, *"an' I'll be right back."*

"Forget it."

As I'm walking off, he calls me back. Brings me over to his car. We get in and drive off, circling around the backstreets of the Cross. He pulls up next to a tired-looking whore lurking outside a McDonald's and she jumps in the backseat. I start to get worried that they are going to rob me. He tells her to get a pipe out, which she does, one of those little numbers fashioned out of a miniature Martell cognac bottle. He pulls over, produces a rock from his mouth, and hands it to me along with the pipe. I unwrap it and place a piece on the gauze, running the flame lightly over it to melt it into place. I take a hit, handing the pipe over as I exhale. It is, at least, real crack. As I blow the crack smoke out the dealer hisses "shit" and I look in the rearview mirror. Police are driving slowly up the street behind us. We are double-parked and the car is literally full of white smoke. He shunts the car into life and starts to drive off as casually as possible while I wrestle with the busted handle to try and wind the window down and let the smoke out.

———

Somehow, when we turn left toward Euston Road again, the cops lose interest and carry on down the street. But now I am nervous as hell and want to get out of the car as fast as possible.

I buy the rock we have been smoking off him and another, bundled up in plastic wrap. In my shaken state I don't take the time to check the merchandise. They drop me off at an amusement arcade on the Caledonian Road. I go into the bathroom and check the second rock. Motherfucker! I realize immediately that I have been burned. A piece of old chewing gum is all that is at the center of the bundle of plastic wrap. I am forty pounds down and I have about ten pounds' worth of crack to show for it.

Stepping out of the bathroom I see someone familiar through the glass front of the arcade, lurking about on the street. With a start, I realize it is Michael. I have not seen him since he threw me out of the place on White Hart Lane. He looks like shit, nervously standing on the corner, waiting for his connection to show up. I have a knife on my belt buckle, and high on that blast of crack I briefly consider sidling up to him and sticking it between his fucking ribs. But fuck it: he already got his. He's back to this tedious fucking routine, just like I am. It seems there is no escape for any of us, whether we have God and the twelve-steps on our side or not.

19

ROUTINE

For the first three months I had to attend Homerton at 9:00 A.M. every morning (except Sundays). I would have my urine tested randomly and would have to drink my entire dose on the premises, supervised by nurses. Then, following the three-month trial period, I was allowed to take a prescription to the chemist. I still had to attend the chemist every day and drink the methadone in clear view of the pharmacist. I had to do it in a chemist more than a mile from my flat, as they were the nearest location that would allow junkies to take their methadone on-site. I learned quickly that administrative quirks like these were the things that could drive an addict to relapse—or insanity—while trying to clean up on methadone. Kids would stare at me as I'd gulp the stuff down, shaking and sick every morning. Their mothers would pull them close. They'd

whisper: "Don't stare—he's a drug addict," if the
kid's gaze rested on me for too long. The chemist,
an old Indian guy called Sanjeep, used to enjoy
my discomfort.

"You don't look so well today, my friend!" he
would boom as I walked in.
All of the eyes in the shop would turn toward me
as I staggered in, pale and unsteady.
"Mary!" he would yell to the old bitch in the back.
"We have another one here for methadone! Fifty
milliliters of linctus please!"

I would smile halfheartedly. It does you no good
to raise your voice or complain. That is the game
they are playing. One angry word from me and he
could ban me from the shop with a single phone
call. Then I am back to going to the hospital every
day for six months before earning the right to
attend the next closest chemist who would dose
me on-site. It is best to shut your mouth and act
with the correct amount of subservience.

After I swallowed the linctus, I would return the
bottle.

"Please to leave the shop," he would say in mangled English, "and not to return until tomorrow.
Thank you."

Liquid Sky's Peel session finally aired on Radio 1.
We all got together at Elektra's house and listened
to it go out live. I left Susan back on Murder Mile,
nodding in front of the television. We drank cheap
champagne and cheered whenever one of our

songs was played. It felt like maybe things would start happening for the band now. I was convinced that after this victory record labels would start calling us with offers. But they never did. The band limped on, waiting for another break, playing gigs in half-empty pubs around North London. Performing such preprogrammed, regimented, electronic music live was a bore, though. I missed the spontaneity of my old bands. Liquid Sky's onstage routine never changed.

Then one night I went over to Elektra's house to work on writing some new songs. She was drunk when I showed up and insisted on pouring me a glassful of vodka. She was already messy, and I could sense that she was working her nerve up to something.

"I like you," she said after an hour or so as we sat around on the floor, programming the new songs on the synthesizer. I looked over at her.

"Yeah . . . I like you too."

"No but . . . I really like you."

"Uh-huh."

I felt my stomach turn to ice. Elektra was my age, but pretty naive. No one in the band knew about my drug use. I knew that it would be a disaster if I started something like this with her. I'd realized that half of the reason I didn't just leave Susan was that she was an insurance of sorts against my having to get emotionally involved with another human being. For someone who didn't like being around other people, Susan was the perfect wife. Our conversations were limited to the bare essentials of our existence: where to find drugs, where to find money. There was no need for any further interaction. I didn't have to hold her, I didn't have to kiss her, I didn't have to fuck her, I didn't have to engage with her on any other level than maybe helping her find a vein when she was too sick to do it herself. But at least I didn't have to consider how alone I was, because when I walked into the apartment there she was—nodded out on the bed or sucking on a cigarette waiting for RJ to call back. Susan was my routine, and now that Elektra was threatening to disrupt it, I felt nothing but unease.

"I don't think this is a good idea." I told Elektra, as nicely as possible.

"Why?" she said, pouting. "Don't you think I'm pretty?"

"Well, yeah . . . but you're married!"

She laughed. "Yeah right! That was to get into the country. I don't love him. He fucks other people. He likes screwing boys in dresses for Christ's sake!"

"Well . . . I'm married, " I bleated.

"And you love her?"

I didn't answer. That lie would have been too preposterous, even for me.

———

"That's what I thought. It's funny how I've never seen you together. Do you keep her in a box?"

Elektra stood up and said, "I'm going to go freshen up." And then she walked to the bathroom, closing the door behind her.

Fuck! Shit, fuck!

As she lingered in the bathroom, my mind whirled. I hadn't had sex in a long, long time. The heroin had killed any urge I once had to fuck. The last time I did it was before Susan and I even got married. With a heroin and crack habit, there was no time for the luxury of having a sex life. I absently wondered if my prick still worked properly. There was something appealing, yet terrifying, about the thought of having sex with Elektra.

But no, it couldn't work. Elektra was a problem because I would have to see her the next day. And the next. And the next. And it would either be incredibly uncomfortable because we'd both regret it the next day or, even worse, she would want us to form some kind of relationship, which was absolutely out of the question. I had too much to hide. Too much that had to remain private.

I needed a shot.

I had a methadone ampoule in my jacket pocket and a new syringe. I went over to the coat rack and retrieved them, stuffing them into my pockets.

The bathroom door opened and Elektra stepped out. Before she could say anything I said, "You mind if I go in there for a moment?" and she nodded me through. I closed the door behind me and stood there for a moment, listening to her walk away into the living room again.

For a minute there was peace. The bathroom was cool and quiet. In the other room I could hear indistinct music playing. I sat down on the toilet, pulling the belt off of my jeans and tossing it onto the floor. I retrieved the needle and the ampoule, snapping the glass neck off the top of the little bottle and sliding the spike into it. I drew up fifty milliliters of clear liquid. Then I had a brain wave.

I had a Ritalin tablet stored away in my jeans. Genius! I squirted the methadone back into the ampoule and retrieved the tablet. I looked around the bathroom for something suitable. There was a glass tumbler by the toothbrushes, so I dried it off with toilet paper and wiped down an area of the tiled floor. I placed the pill on the floor and used the bottom of the glass like a mortar and pestle to crush the pill up into rough white powder. Then I used an old underground ticket to scoop up the powder and dump it into the cup. I sucked up the methadone once more and squirted it into the cup, swirling the solution until it turned thick and creamy.

This was a dangerous practice. Shooting pills can really fuck up your veins and cause all kinds of nasty medical problems. Normally I would take the time to filter and refilter the solution, but I realized that I was taking a long time in the bathroom, so after a quick swirl with the plunger of the syringe, I sucked the creamy, lumpy solution up, clasped the needle between my teeth, and started wrapping my belt around my upper arm.

I went in by the side of my forearm. I slid in the needle in and poked around under the skin, drilling for blood. There was nothing, but when I withdrew the needle a great glob of crimson bubbled out of my arm and started running toward my wrist. I wiped the blood with my hand, smearing it all over myself in an attempt to stop it from dripping on the floor. Then, flexing again, I pointed my clenched fist toward the floor in an attempt to increase the blood flow and inserted the needle into my wrist.

This was a tricky operation. Shooting anywhere around the tendons is a problem because if the needle accidentally sticks one you know about it. An explosion of pain and even the loss of sensation in one or more of your fingers for an anxious half hour can result. But there are a lot of decent veins hiding there, just under the surface. A thin strip of blood shot into the barrel, turning the solution pink, and I started to feed it in slowly, but the needle immediately jammed.

"Fuck!" I hissed. This was the problem with injecting inadequately filtered crushed tablets. I pulled the needle out and more blood gushed from the wrist, this time splashing the floor. I had blood all over my hands and my forearm now, and a little pool of it at my feet. I slid the needle in the same spot again, knowing that if I didn't get the hit straight away now the needle would clog and the entire shot would be wasted.

I said a silent prayer to the God of junkies, and by divine intervention, a plume of scarlet flooded the barrel and I started depressing the plunger and feeding the shot into my vein. I was so caught up in the process that I didn't even hear the bathroom door open. The Ritalin and methadone hit my bloodstream and almost exactly on cue Elektra screamed, "What the fuck are you doing?!?"

I looked up and saw her standing there wearing just a T-shirt. I sat stupefied by the sight of her bare legs, the tuft of pubic hair sticking out from under the shirt, and the look of horror on her face, before I jumped up, with the needle still hanging out of my wrist, and yelled, *"Close the door!"* She slammed it closed, and I was alone once more. I put the cap back on the needle and stashed it, gathering up my things, looping the belt back into my jeans, and cleaning up the blood with a thick wad of wet toilet paper. All the while the blood was roaring in my ears from the shot and my vision kept blurring in and out.

"What kind of person doesn't have a lock on their bathroom door, anyway?" I thought bitterly, flushing the toilet and straightening myself up in the mirror. When I left the bathroom, Elektra had pulled on a pair of tights to cover herself a little and was sitting on the couch, shakily drinking another vodka. I popped my head in and said: "Look, I'm sorry. You really didn't know?"

———

She looked up and shook her head.

"Well, I'm sorry you had to see that. I'd better go. I'll call you tomorrow."

She nodded. She looked completely freaked out by what she had just witnessed in her bathroom. I grabbed my coat and got the fuck out of there.

20

DR. IRA

Tuesdays—I meet with Dr. Ira in Hackney, East London, to ensure that the flow of methadone remains uninterrupted. Methadone gives and methadone takes away—rather like God, in a way. If methadone is God then Dr. Ira is His gin-soaked St. Peter, sitting at the gates, checking boxes, deciding if I have been naughty or nice in the week since he last passed judgment on me.

Sterile, airless atmosphere in the waiting room. Smell of detergent and junk sickness wafting out from aching muscles and creaking bones. Old woman behind the reception desk with a white, starched, severe face eyes me with obvious conde-scension. The good doctor owns me, for all intents and purposes. I am sure the pursed-lipped old receptionists and nurses are in love with Dr. Ira's twisted pipe-tobacco-stained old bones in their own dried-up, pent-up way.

———

Dr. Ira is a repulsive old specimen.

Stink of professional arrogance and brandy all over his sweating, leering, ruptured old face. After thirty years in the service, junkies are his life now. He has the same love-hate ambivalence toward us as we have toward the drugs that constitute our lives.

"Fuck Hannah," a male voice says from behind me.

"Martin," says a shrill East End harpy, "she's pregnant. We can't leave her wivout nothing."

"That fucking cunt will take all of our fucking gear and leave us sick. She's a fucking liberty taker. Fuck her and that fucking fetus she's dragging around."

"Martin—she's all right—you've got her all wrong."

"No I fucking don't! Tell her she can't fucking crash with us. Who knocked her up, anyway?"

"Denzil."

"That paki cunt? Tell her to stay with that fucking bastard then!"

"He fucking raped her. She can't stay wiv him."

"Raped her, my arse. She fucked him for rock. She'd fuck anyone for rock."

———

"I know she would. But that sick cunt raped her."

"Did he give her a pipe?"

"Well, yeah, but—"

"Then she fucked him for rock. End of."

The East End harpy has her blond hair, black at the roots, tied back in a severe bun. It is pulled back so tight that it accentuates the harsh contours of her skull. She has a black eye that has faded to the color of autumn leaves. Her boyfriend is a skeletal old jailbird, bathed in sticky coagulating withdrawal sweat. He nervously clenches and unclenches his inked fists and stares at the polished tile floor.

Last night I had a dream that Dr. Ira told me to suck my methadone out of a rubber phallus protruding from the fly of his dandruff-sprinkled brown slacks. It was part of my treatment plan, he told me, laughing.

In the dream, I did it.

Wouldn't you?

"Now," Dr. Ira is saying to me, rustling his papers up and down and coughing phlegm into his palm, "take those *child molesters,* hum? They say that they can't help it. Chemical castration doesn't help. It's a medical condition that they have. There aren't many reformed child molesters out there."

———

The child molester speech. I hate the way his lips seem to grow wetter and thicker, redder and mushier, when he talks about child molestation.

"There is evidence to suggest their claim that they *can't* stop what they are doing. But your claims that you can't stop . . . well, frankly my boy . . . they are contraindicated."

"And how is that, Dr. Ira?"

"Well, because there are *innumerable* ex-addicts out there. They are legion."

"You mean the God-botherers."

Dr. Ira smiles his practiced old predator's smile.

"Well, yes, the Narcotics Anonymous people, of course. But others also."

"And how long do they stay clean?" I ask. "I mean, when do you consider them clean? After a year? Two years? Five?"

"Any time away from drugs would be considered a period of clean time."

"But *how long* do they stay clean for?"

It is the old chicken-and-egg scenario that we always get into. This is the game. Dr. Ira wants me to reduce my methadone. Even if I were to reduce it by just five milliliters, he would be happy. In reality, if I reduced by five milliliters a day I would not feel the deficit. But once I reduce, there will be no way—bar buying the methadone off the black market—for me to ever get my dose put back up. It will never happen. The inflexible authority of the clinic can never be overexaggerated.

If I remain at Homerton Drug Dependency Unit for twenty years on a methadone program, never again use street drugs, hold down a job, buy a house, start a family—all of that kind of happy shite—I will still be considered a failure for Dr. Ira. For me to qualify as a success to his superiors, I must reduce my dose over a period of time until I am opiate-free, allowing me to leave the program. If I do that, but then return to using street drugs and eventually kill some old bastard for his pension money so I can score, I will still be considered a roaring success by the hospital's standards. There is no follow-up treatment. As soon as I walk out the door—clean, for however short a period—I am judged a success.

So we carry on this dance, week after week. Dr. Ira gives me his little speeches. I listen, respectfully decline his offers of dose reduction, and walk out with a prescription for one week's supply of methadone. And then it starts all over again.

My daily routine has evolved over the past year. Today I receive my prescription once a week, take it to a chemist, and then return every morning to the same chemist to pick up a bottle of sticky, sickly sweet methadone linctus. I can take the bottle home and use it whenever I need it. I can save it up and use heroin instead. I have approximately two thousand milliliters, stored in medicine bottles around my flat. It makes me feel secure. The King of Purgatory, with all of his adornments.

After six months at Homerton I underwent my review. No dirty urines. This was quite simple to achieve. For that whole period I was piss tested regularly, observed by a nurse. So I injected black-market methadone, the kind that comes in ampoules specifically for that purpose. It is impossible to get by prescription unless you have a private doctor. The only way most junkies can afford a private doctor is to play up their habit and sell the excess ampoules. It was a shitty high, but better than nothing. After three months I was allowed to piss alone. Then I used other people's piss.

Most opiates are out of the bloodstream in three days. At the clinic people would take turns using heroin or staying off. After three days off, they were pissing good, clean urine again. Then they filled up a bottle and distributed it to everyone else they were friendly with. Everybody involved could use heroin most of the time and pass the urine test all of the time. After the first six months, the piss tests became less regular, so as long as I was careful I could do as I pleased. It is all about working the angles at the methadone clinics.

Does Dr. Ira believe I have been off heroin for a year? No. Does he believe any of his patients have? No. Does he care, as long as he doesn't have to explain the dirty urine samples to *his* higher-ups?

———

No, no, and no.

Walking out of the clinic with my prescription I feel like a lottery winner. The bastards are off my back for another seven days. Back to Murder Mile, Susan, and my cold-water flat. Back to the old gray-haired pharmacist and the old black cleaner Leroy, who walks around the shop floor dazed, broom in hand. There are more shootings per capita on Murder Mile than anywhere else in Great Britain. The drug trade is to blame, mostly the Yardies who control the crack trade. Scoring crack around Upper Clapton can be a risky business. Junkies can get caught in the cross fire of turf wars and displays of machismo. DC, a young kid I bought from on occasion, was found dead in the back of an abandoned Vauxhall Astra last month. One day his mobile was turned off and then a day later I saw it on the news: another dead kid on Murder Mile. Turns out he was fourteen. I remember absently thinking that kids are looking older these days. I suppose a gun and a bag of rocks can make anyone look like a man in poor light.

21

JANUARY, AGAIN

I am watching Susan sleep.

I am wondering, If I killed her now, would I get away with it? Susan looks dead already. When she sleeps, she looks like a corpse. She smells like a corpse too. Maybe she would thank me for it.

I realize that if I could make Susan just . . . disappear . . . no questions asked, I would do it in an instant.

Or would I?

It always comes back to drugs. As a woman, Susan is useful for certain things. I know that she is able to wheedle credit out of RJ in a way that I would never be able to. Because she can make herself seem pathetic, wounded, and in need of help.

That's Susan's whole deal, the only card she has to play. But it still works on people. There have been times when there has been no more money for dope, no way of getting dope, and Susan has come through for us. They are rare occurrences, but they have happened nonetheless.

But what am I going to do with Susan in the long term? I cannot remember the last time we fucked. The idea fills me with an uneasy revulsion. Susan was no beauty when I met her, and in the intervening few years she has bankrupted herself completely. She looks ancient, worn-out, a shell of who she used to be. I look at myself in the mirror and can still see traces of the old me. I wonder if Susan sees that when she looks at herself. I think that she must. Someone as insecure as Susan, if she saw what I saw, maybe she would take her own life. Heroin is cruel to women, I think, crueler than it is to men. Male junkies take on a certain look, a certain starved appearance around the cheeks and the jawline, but on women it has the effect of making them look uglier, haggard, mean. In the long run, there are no beautiful female junkies. Even Nico, poor beautiful Nico, wore her face out toward the end. And she was starting from a position of breathtaking gorgeousness. For Susan there was no chance.

I am a coward. I do not have the nerve to kill Susan. I am just indulging in fanciful thoughts because she is passed out and I am awake. Shit, if I didn't have the nerve to leave her, where would I find the nerve to kill her? Sometimes she says things like: "If I hadn't found heroin, I think I would have killed myself."

Other times she says: "If you weren't around, I think I'd do it. I'd get it over with."

How am I supposed to respond to that? Susan is twelve years older than me. She must know that I will not be around forever. I just mumble shit like "Don't talk like that."

I have seen Susan high on Xanax, back in LA, holding a loaded handgun under her chin. Her eyes wet. We had reached the end of the line again when we were staying in her mother's house in Venice. Her stepfather kept a gun underneath his bookshelf. She knew, and one night when we were alone there she took it out and placed the gun under her chin. I watched her, frozen.

"Is that thing loaded?" I asked her eventually.

"Yes. What use is an unloaded gun?"

I nodded. There were no more drugs. We couldn't stay clean.

"I'm tired," she said.

"Me too. I'm tired too."

"I can't do it," she said eventually. She handed the gun to me. It felt heavy. She said: "Put it in my mouth."

———

She opened her mouth. I put the gun in her mouth. She closed her eyes like she was in prayer. I held it there for a few moments, and then, defeated, I withdrew the gun from her mouth. I knew what she wanted me to do, but I couldn't do it. I handed the gun back to her and told her that I was sorry.

She placed the gun back under her chin.

"I want to do it. I'm fucking serious this time. I really want to do it. Would you do it if I did it first?"

"Put the gun down," I told her. "Don't be so fucking stupid. There's always more drugs. More time. This isn't the way."

The next day she left for rehab on her father's insurance, and I wound up in a sober-living house. But I never forgot that incident.

It hung over me, an implied threat that if I ever left, I would be pulling the trigger that I chickened out of pulling that night.

Susan was still asleep. There was nothing to be done. I sat by the window and waited for dawn.

22

ST. STEVEN

I occasionally returned to the Virgin Megastore to shoplift after being let go from my job there all those months ago. I knew the positioning of the security cameras and that the security staff were lazy, fat, ignorant, and complacent. It was simply a matter of learning how to remove the security cases quickly and discreetly. I learned the technique from Steve Cook. Steve had an almost Zen approach to stealing. He had a lizardlike calm and an economy of movement that I have never seen equaled before or since. He could locate the weak spots in the square plastic security boxes and crack them open with an almost undetectable application of pressure with the thumbs. The case would fall away like an old chrysalis and the CD would slide into his pocket as if it had never been there. Of all the times that Steve had been in prison, it had never once been for shoplifting.

———

But, like so many others in my life, one day he simply wasn't there anymore. His phone was cut off; there was no one at his house, the curtains were drawn, and the place was shrouded in darkness. Gone. I realized that I did not know his family, or anyone outside of the circle of people we scored or used drugs with, and none of them had a clue. Maybe back inside Wormwood Scrubs for a spell. Maybe dead from bad drugs or an unpaid debt. Steve was a father; his two children lived with their mother. I sometimes smiled and thought about how wonderful it would be to have a father as knowledgeable and cunning as Steve.

The image of Steve that I would take with me was in Steve's kitchen in his council flat in Dagenham. We had just returned there from seeing his connection at a working man's club hidden away in a council estate, talking football and politics with the cab driver, who obviously knew that we were buying drugs but didn't care, and then stumbling dizzily back into the flat, blinds drawn and music on—*Deserter's Songs* by Mercury Rev—and Steve said, "This bastard's voice is a bit fruity but he has *something*," and I wondered if that album could be summed up any better by anyone.

And the sickness fell away from us as we cooked the junk and prepared the pipes. The first order of business was to get well and Steve had a knack for finding veins in the most abused and calcified of areas and offered to help me shoot. He found blood with a surgeon's precision—sheen of clear perspiration on his forehead—and, saintlike, he rolled up his sleeve and took his own shot second.

And in the kitchen with the smack taking me, I looked at Steve—his skinny arms and rib cage poking out like the angles of a Schiele self-portrait—and the spike threaded into his arm and he *tap-tap-tapped* the syringe like he was checking the wall for hollow spots, and with an almost audible *pop* the needle burst through the vein and dark red blood lazily flowed into the syringe, turning the heroin black.

And this was it—this was beauty—no sickness, no worries, no nothing, except friends and the safety of heroin and the crack we were about to smoke and a whole day to waste—nothing but days and days and weeks to waste—no matter, life could not intrude into this sacred space.

I feel an understanding of God that I have never felt before, I thought as Steve pushed the hit into his vein in much the same way that Jesus might have, and we connected with something larger and more ancient and more vast than either of us could truly conceive of before the drugs.

Adios, Steve. Life had become a series of revolving faces, careering from medical emergency to drug spin out, from arrests to rehab, from relapse to sudden death or disappearance.

———

In my run-down flat in Murder Mile I said a prayer to Steve. I lay still on the collapsing bed and laid my arms out in a cruciform. On the CD player Ornate Coleman played—the sacred and the profane—while I waited, looking out the window to the overcast East London sky, waiting for something, anything, to happen.

23

JOBS (PORNO)

Money was low. I had taken all of my checks to various backstreet check-cashing joints all over the city. They often had to be sought out. Fabric stores, shoe shops, and vendors of cheap, imported tourist trinkets were always a good bet. "Payday Advance" was the most commonly used euphemism.

Soon after receiving my last illicit ninety-three pounds from one of these transactions, I decided to see if my card would bear the cost of one more travel card for the underground. As soon as I slipped the useless strip of plastic into the machine, the screen blinked up RETAINED—RETAINED—CONTACT YOUR BANK OR FINANCIAL INSTITUTION. I hopped the turnstile with my last forty quid in my pocket and vowed to find another source of income.

———

WANTED. SALESPERSON. ADULT ENTER-
TAINMENT / BOOKSTORE. OVER 18 ONLY.
NO CRIMINAL RECORDS. 15 P.H. CALL MICK.

Well, shit. There was money to be made in porno.
Back in LA I had gotten paid $50 when I really
needed money for dope to be an extra in a porno
flick called *Snatch Adams*. The shoot had taken
place in an abandoned hospital in a run-down
neighborhood called Boyle Heights. I went along
with a guy I knew from the methadone clinic
called Speedball Eddie, who did this kind of shit
as a profession of sorts. He would fill in as an audience member for any and all of the crap that was
filmed in LA: *Judge Judy, The People's Court, Rosie
O'Donnell*, whatever. He'd make his dope money
by just sitting there, clapping maniacally whenever the "APPLAUSE" light went on. Sometimes
I'd catch a glimpse of him on my little portable
TV, with his lopsided, self-administered Beatles
haircut and his wide, brown, burn-out eyes, clapping like a seal for his fifty dollars, while more
mundane human dramas than his own played out
on-screen.

I thought the shoot might be kind of fun, but it
wasn't. It was odd and creepy. I was skagged out
of my mind and so nothing really turned me on
anymore. The hospital itself was like something
out of some cheesy "after the apocalypse" kind of
movie. The place was in total disarray: glass cabi-
nets hung open as if people had looted the place
and fled, gang graffiti covered a lot of the walls.
Wandering the halls, Eddie and I came across

room after room, each more forlorn and desolate than the last . . . overturned institutional tables . . . metal stretchers with frayed and worn leather restraints . . . trays of rusted, unusable, obscure medical instruments . . . it was possibly the coldest, least inviting place on the planet.

Our scene lasted less than a few moments. They filmed it at 11:30 in the morning. On a dirty-looking hospital bed, a blond, plastic-looking girl in a nurse's uniform was being fucked by two guys. The director kept stopping and repositioning them, and then they'd carry on as if nothing had happened.

"Yeah . . . take it you fucking bitch!"

"Oh . . . Right there. . . . Faster . . ."

On cue, Speedball Eddie and I walked past the scene in white doctor's coats. We paused, looked over at the action on the bed, and, unfazed by the sight of the woman getting screwed from behind as she sucked the other guy's oddly oversized cock, we nodded to each other, made notes on our clipboards, and walked on. We were so close to them, you could smell the sex. And we had earned our fifty bucks, just like that. They actually offered Eddie an extra seventy-five if he would take part in a gangbang, but it would involve hanging around till 6:00 P.M., and Eddie had people to see. Despite the fact I would have turned down the money also, I was privately a little offended that they didn't ask me as well.

———

So there was no embarrassment in my showing up for the interview for the porno store. When I called, Mick grilled me over the phone, mostly about whether I had a criminal record. When I insisted for the third time that I didn't have one of any kind, he relented and told me to stop by the shop for an interview.

The store was on Wardour Street, the heart of the Soho porn trade. For a while it was the only place in the whole of the UK where you could buy hardcore porn legally. When the Internet rendered such laws obsolete, hardcore finally arrived in the provinces, but the porno trade is still one of the most thriving businesses in Soho, alongside prostitution, drugs, and trendy wine bars. I showed up five minutes early. Mick was still with the interviewee before me. The store was being watched by two kids, who looked like typical council estate boys—white trainers, chunky gold jewelry, cropped hair gelled tightly to their heads, bulldog tattoos and tracksuits.

"I'm here for the interview."

"All right mate. 'E's in the back right now. 'Ave a browse and 'e'll be out in a bit."

It was pretty typical fare. Dildos of varying shapes and sizes lined one wall. Magazines, with names like *Color Climax, Euro Sluts,* and *Backdoor Beauties* filled the center aisles. The other wall was covered in DVDs. In England, there is still a furtive feel to porno shops. It is how I imagine a liquor store in Utah would feel. There is a sense that what people here are doing *is* legal, but still beyond the pale and rather degenerate. A few embarrassed-looking customers shuffled in while I was browsing, men who refused to make eye contact with each other and who bristled with discomfort when the kids in the tracksuits threw out a casual "All right mate?" in their directions. A door against the back wall opened, and a big guy with a beard walked out, followed by the other guy there for the interview. He was wearing a dirty-looking T-shirt and jeans. I had at least made the effort to wear a shirt. Well shit, this asshole probably didn't need the job as badly as I did. I nodded at the fat bastard with a beard and he introduced himself as Mick.

"Step into my office."

The office turned out to be a stockroom, and a small one at that. It was stuffed with magazines and DVDs. Everywhere you looked there were spread cunts, asses, tits, and more erect cocks than I had probably seen in my entire life. The room was crammed and airless. Oh Christ, what if I got the job? I couldn't turn it down, I needed the cash badly. But the reality of working in this store started to cut through even the insulation of the methadone I had injected before showing up and I started to feel claustrophobic and sick.

"Nice guy," Mick said, by way of introduction. "I would have given 'im the job too. He's done this kind of thing before. But he had a criminal record. Can't hire someone with a criminal record. Do you have a criminal record?"

———

"No," I told him, again.

"I mean, it's not that I give a shit what anyone's done in the past, right? It's the fucking council. They're all over this trade. They'd close us down if they could. They control it from the fucking ground up! Basically, if you take this job, you're working for Westminster Council. That's why I have to ask. Fill this in, will you? I'll be right back."

He handed me a blurry, photocopied form. It had only a handful of questions: name, date of birth, national insurance number, address, and, finally, "Do you have a criminal record—y/n?" and he left me alone. I filled out the form and waited for Mick to return. On the shelf above me, a huge pink dildo poked out over my head like the sword of Damocles.

Dave came back in and gave my application form a cursory glance, before placing it on his desk. "You done this kind of work before?"

"Well, shop work, yeah. I know how to work a till. But it's been off-licenses and music shops. Not porn."

"That's all right. Here, I want you to take a look at something."

He pulled a magazine from a pile on his desk. It was called *Anal Cream Pies*. I looked at the cover, which showed a close-up of a red-looking anus with a huge drip of semen hanging from it. Next to the ass was a blond girl with an extended tongue. She was winking at the camera as the cum leaked from the ass onto her tongue. It wasn't quite embarrassment that I felt. It was an oddly disassociated feeling. It was the oddness of the situation that was the worst—pawing through a hardcore porn mag, in a tiny stockroom, with a big sweaty bearded guy called Mick all but sitting on my knee. By my standards, I'll admit, it was pretty tame. In LA I had injected enough meth and smoked enough crack that I had found myself in plenty more bizarre situations than this. Still, it wasn't Sunday school.

"Take a look inside," Mick instructed.

I did. The front cover had pretty much said it all, to be honest. The magazine consisted of photosets, all telling the story of how a young woman—or a pair of young women—end up getting an anus full of semen. Each picture had a caption in German, Spanish, French, and oddly translated English: *"Pretty Anna is surprised by presences of her boss Duke, in the after hours of the office. 'Oh' says Anna 'I thought you had left, Duke!' . . . 'Not yet. You and your sweet little ass are burning the midnight oils I can see,' Duke sneers, loosening his belt."*

"Does it offend you? The magazine? Cos it's exactly the kind of thing we sell here."

"Well, the grammar's a little offensive. But apart from that . . . no."

"The grammar? How'd you mean?"

"The little bits of story they have under here. Does anybody actually read that?"

"I've never given it much thought."

I handed the magazine back to Mick. He looked at me with a sardonic grin. I started to worry that he thought I was trying to be a smart arse. I needed the job. Fuck. If I didn't get it, no rent, no drugs. Rent I could deal with, except without a fixed address I stood to lose my methadone script, which didn't bear thinking about. I decided to shut the fuck up and speak when spoken to.

"Okay. Lets role play," Dave said, leaning forward.

"Sure."

"A geezer comes in, right? And he wants a contact mag. D'you know what a contact mag is? It's a mag that carries adverts for people who want to meet up for sex. Men looking for women. Women for men. Men for men. Women for women. Men for sheep. You get the idea, right?"

"Yes."

"And he needs one for, say, West London. He's looking for a dominatrix in West London. Right?"

"Right."

———

"But we only have a mag that deals with piss drinkers in South London."

"Erm . . . yes . . ."

"Do you tell him to come back when the mag is in stock next week? Or do you just sell him the piss drinker contact mag for South London regardless?"

I knew where this was going. This was just another "fuck the mooch over for money" gig. This I could deal with. This interview I could nail.

"I'd sell him what we have in stock," I tell Mick. "Don't let 'em walk out without buying something."

"Good!"

Fuck it was hot in there. And small. I could hear the bastard breathing in and out.

"Okay, here's another one. Let me show you this. . . ."
He rummaged though the junk on his desk again, this time coming up with a small bottle of clear liquid.

"Spanish fly," he informed me with a leer, handing the little bottle over for me to look at. It reminded me of those little bottles of amyl nitrate I used to sniff to get high when I was younger. "You know what Spanish fly is?"

———

"Sure."

"This is the original, mate. Before all of that Via-gra rubbish. Spanish fly keeps you hard for hours and drives the women mental. Thirty quid a bot-tle, that goes for. It's the pheromones, you see?"

I looked the unassuming bottle over again. It seemed inconceivable that grown men could fall for shit like this.

"Would you still sell this," Mick continued, "if I told you that there was nothing more potent than ginger ale in that bottle?"

"Sure. Why not?"

"Right answer!"

Mick leaned over and shook my hand.
"I have one more geezer to see today, so I'll give you a call in the afternoon. Thanks for your time."

"No problem."

"Hey, before you go . . . could I interest you in some Spanish fly? Drives the women crazy!"
He cackled his dirty smoker's laugh again, and I told him, "I think I'll pass, thanks." Walking out of the shop and into a Soho afternoon, I felt gripped by the complete patheticness of my situ-ation. In six years I had gone from someone who had just gotten signed to a major record label,

embarked on a world tour, and been on the verge of truly great things to a penniless junkie, banking on getting a job in a Soho porn shop so I could earn enough to feed my habit. I started to laugh a little, but it was a sad kind of laugh so I stopped again. It sounded stilted, forced, and ugly as it bounced off the bricks of Walker's Court.

24

SECOND CHANCES

April Fools' Day. Suddenly and gloriously, I found myself in a band again. I answered an ad in the *New Musical Express* for a signed band looking for a keyboardist, left a message, and was called back a week later and told to show up to a studio by Old Street station for a tryout. I had also received a call back about the porno store. They wanted me to start the following week, and I wasn't in a position to turn the job down. My hours would be twelve noon to twelve midnight, four days a week. I imagined looking at all of those dildos and latex vaginas and inflatable sex dolls for twelve hours a day and realized that I might go insane, and this focused my energy even more on scoring this gig. I turned up to the tryout glowing with methadone and focused. This gig was important because the band in question was signed to an actual record label. The artist was Kelly Leyton, the one-time vocalist with a hugely successful trip-hop group called the Trainer Whores now embarking on a solo career. The album was in the can and about to be released, with "much fanfare" as her manager promised on the phone. There was a tour in support of a successful rock act called Garbage already booked to begin in two weeks, so I went to the rehearsal in the mood to take no prisoners.

I was introduced to the rest of the band, and then we ran through the songs I had learned from the CD I had received in the post the previous week. I had practiced diligently and brought all of myself into the room this time. No stashed syringes of methadone or heroin. No cocaine, no crack. Just me, and whatever I hadn't lost in the intervening years.

After the rehearsal I was immediately offered the slot. I had felt it in my gut. The chemistry was there. The music I produced meshed with what the band was doing. I actually enjoyed myself for the first time in years. Kelly claimed to have psychic abilities and she placed her hand on me for a second and then smiled. It seemed that the vibes were right. I also met the manager, Alex. He was a chubby, boyish man with a bowl haircut and red cheeks. He seemed like a pussycat compared to other managers I had been involved with in the past.

"It's great to have you onboard!" he said, shaking my hand furiously.

"It's great to be onboard!"

———

"This is just the beginning. I'm in the process of booking more dates to support the album's release. We'll be quite busy. The Garbage tour is just the beginning!"

Walking home from the rehearsal, I allowed myself to gloat a little. It was actually happening again. I was signed to a record label. I could go back to doing what I did best, before I ruined it all with the drugs. I started to think that if I could just bank on this one thing working out okay, it could be a comeback that Lazarus would be envious of.

It took me a week of negotiations back and forth with the clinic before I realized that there was no way that they would let me pick up a week's worth of methadone. Dr. Ira seemed to relish delivering the deathblow.

"I understand, that this . . . tour . . . constitutes some kind of opportunity for you. But I simply cannot let you walk out of here with a prescription for that much methadone. Any other answer, I'm afraid, would be . . . unprofessional."

So I had to buy my medication on the black market. Forty pounds got me enough methadone linctus for the week, which I measured out into the correct doses and took with me in a mouthwash bottle. For all of the efforts of doctors like Ira, black-market methadone was readily available all over the city. On the corner of Tottenham Court Road and Oxford Street, between certain

times and on certain days, if you had the right
kind of face, you could score methadone juice or
ampoules from the old junkies who congregated
outside the underground station. I often found
myself ghosting around Soho scoring Physeptone
tablets from the relics of the West End's old junk-
dealing scene, survivors of the golden days when
you could buy Chinese heroin from the old push-
ers who lurked by the restaurants and Laundromats of Chinatown, then on to Lady Frankau's
for a prescription for pure coke and morphine.
They lurked around the corners, in the alleyways
and shop doorways, huddling in their jackets and
eyeing the passersby with cold, hungry eyes.

The band met up at the rehearsal room one last
time before we were to start the tour. This was
when we met our tour manager for the first time.
He was a handsome, boyish-looking man with
tousled hair who staggered in fifteen minutes
late, obviously severely hungover and a little
befuddled.

"All right loves!" he yelled. "Sorry I'm late. Had a
bit of trouble with my phone."

"You got it fixed?" Alex asked, in an attempt at
sounding managerial.

"Well, not quite. It's at the bottom of a canal. But
no worries, it's all under control!"

He was called Dan. And over the next few weeks
I came to consider him a real friend.

———

As I left London, Susan, the methadone clinics, and Murder Mile behind, all of it fading away as we tore up the M1, barreling on to new cities, new landscapes, new people, I felt myself expanding to fit the air that was suddenly all around me, and the remembrance of who I once was came flooding to my mind.

The idea of me at eighteen years old, with friends who would soon be torn from me by circumstance and time, but who at this moment were my entire world . . . the idea of me being someone at the beginning of a journey, rather than limping toward it's conclusion defeated . . . the idea of my having ambitions beyond simply getting enough money to pay rent this week and getting some heroin into my blood started to become something other than an abstract notion. . . . It became something almost tangible for the first time in years.

And as the bus lurched toward the first stop on the tour, I felt a surge of almost forgotten, but still familiar, emotions filling my brain, as if I were a waking coma victim. I looked to my travel bag stuffed under my seat, knowing that it contained a Listerine bottle filled with enough methadone to kill every man and woman on this bus, and I wondered if I were to toss it out the window onto the asphalt that zoomed past underneath us, would I—this newly awakened I—even feel the sickness anymore?

The shows flew by in a dizzying sugar rush. In every city we landed from Bristol to Edinburgh,

Dan had a connection for cocaine, and the tour bus was in a blizzard of it; and, as is usual on tour, it was the lighting guys, the guitar techs, and the guys who operated the mixing desk who partied harder than the band. Having stopped drinking totally since starting using heroin, I suddenly began consuming great oceans of booze. The guitar tech was an old speed freak called Pat, who started selling me Dexedrine tablets, which I swallowed before every show. For the duration of the tour, I was indestructible. Superhuman. Before the shows I would vanish with Dan into the underbelly of whatever city we were in to score cocaine. We bought from shady men with faded blue prison tattoos and gold jewelry in high-rise council blocks, from Arabs who moved the stuff from under the counters of their side-street kebab shops, and from one guy in Newcastle who had a nice middle-class home, a wife, and two young children running about the place. All of them were on first-name terms with our tour manager. I started to feel an affinity toward Dan that I hadn't felt for another human being in a long time.

One night, following a drunken show in Edinburgh, I slipped his mobile phone from his jacket pocket and started drunkenly calling numbers stored within it. He walked in on me, huddled in the back of the tour bus, talking dirty to a girl called Vanessa I had chosen at random from his address book. Instead of hanging up, she had encouraged it, and the whole thing went on for at least fifteen minutes. Dan walked in, saw me on his phone talking to one of his friends about eating her pussy, and snatched the phone from my hand.

"No . . . no," he said to her, "that's just one of the alcoholics we have in the band. I know, love. He's incorrigible."

The next morning I woke up, staggered from the bunk of the tour bus, and ran to the exit. I threw open the door just in time to vomit violently onto the concrete below. Looking up, I saw all of Garbage and most of their crew, who happened to be walking past at the exact moment that the puke erupted from me. They stopped and half-smiled. Shirley Manson looked impossibly small next to the crew of ex-Marines the band had carting their equipment around for them. I grinned at her and said as cheerfully as I could, "Lovely morning!" giving a friendly wave. They carried on walking.

25

VANESSA

The final show. We walked offstage and into the dressing room, the yells of the crowd bouncing off the walls like the bloody yelps of spectators at a cockfight. The show was a success. You could hear a hush descend slightly as the audience realized that now that we had vacated the stage Garbage was preparing to make their appearance. Kelly hugged each member of the band in turn.

"Well done, mate," she told each of us.

There was a twinge of sadness that it was over. It seemed so anticlimactic to go back to my flat after a week of carefree living on a bus. Even being in the little bunk bed above our drummer, Chris, sleeping in a little darkened coffin-space as we drove all night from city to city, seemed much more appealing than another night in my own bed. I opened a beer, took a last look around the dressing room, and said to Chris: "Let's go check what's happening in the audience."

We walked through the back tunnels of Brixton Academy and made our way to the VIP area, which was a room above the audience with TV monitors to show the performance in close-up and a huge glass window looking down on the stage. I looked around. There was Susan, with some girl from the methadone clinic she had obviously started hanging around with. The pair of them looked like they had wandered in from the street. I walked over and said hey.

"Hey," Susan said, pointing to her friend, "this is Julie."

"Hi, Julie."

"Nice show. Well done."

"Thanks."

Then the three of us sank into silence for a moment.

"We were just saying," Julie said, breaking in, "I know a geezer round here called Ahmed who's had some pretty good gear recently. You want to come over to his place? He's close by, like."

"Well, maybe later. I have to speak to people, you know."

———

"Oh yeah, right. No worries."

"D'you want to go now, and we can come back?" Susan asked Julie.

"Well . . . if you don't mind. Before it gets too late. . . ."

I felt a flood of relief. I had never felt it before, and as it happened I immediately felt like an asshole, but I suddenly became embarrassed by being seen around Susan. I silently cursed her! She hadn't even made the effort to clean herself up. Her hair was unwashed and sticking up in clumps on her head. She looked like she had just rolled out of bed so she could head out to score. Although I had managed to downplay my drug dependence to everyone in the band, I realized that as soon as they got a look at Susan they would have to know that something was up. The girl had junkie written all over her. Her face was sunken in, her pupils barely there. She had obviously bathed herself in thick, pungent perfume to cover up her stink rather than subject herself to a shower. Since becoming an addict, I had become something of a stranger to personal hygiene myself, but when I was in close proximity to straight people I at least made the effort to try and wash some of the stench off me. I hurried the pair of them toward the exit and told Susan I would call her to tell her where the after-party would be.

Walking back into the VIP room I saw Dan deep in conversation with a girl. Well, I noticed the girl first. She was olive-skinned and beautiful, with striking cheekbones and full, red lips. She seemed somehow apart from everyone else in the room. It was in the way she stood, the way she dressed. It was as if everyone else in the place were in black and white and she was the only one in color. Suddenly, I felt nervous. It was the kind of nervousness that I hadn't felt in a long time and it took me by surprise. Dan saw me staring at them and beckoned me over.

He smiled at me broadly as I walked over to them. I stared at her face as I approached. I couldn't help it. I had never seen anyone like her. She had the most beautiful lips, and perfect, dark eyes. She looked like she was inwardly laughing at me.

"You finally get to meet!" Dan grinned as I walked over and said hello. I didn't understand.

"Finally?"

"Oh, you remember," the girl said, and as soon as she opened her mouth to speak I knew. I knew immediately who it was and there was embarrassment for sure, but also a curious kind of sexual thrill that this girl was the one . . . "I believe you were going to bend me over and stick it into me from behind?"

"I'll leave you two to get acquainted." Dan laughed, splitting the scene, leaving us there in the dull light, regarding each other.

We smiled, but surprisingly there was no awkwardness. I did not feel self-conscious in the slightest. In fact, for a reason that I could not immediately fathom, I was brimming over with carefree self-confidence, as if I were eighteen and still vibrating from my first ever line of cocaine.

"I'm sorry for the obscene phone call," I told her. "I was drunk and feeling mischievous."

She smiled. "Don't worry. I've heard worse. I'm from New York—you'd have to work hard to shock me."

The conversation flowed easily. We talked about music, art, and books. We seemed to share all of the same reference points, which was a disconcerting experience. Vanessa was a fascinating girl. She grew up surrounded by the beauty and insanity of New York City, an Ecuadorian punk-rock kid from Queens who cut her teeth on the Lower East Side's hardcore and punk scenes . . . sipping Ballantine Ale and skipping homework to catch the Ramones at the Ritz, slam-dancing to the Circle Jerks at CBGB's Sunday hardcore matinee, before graduating to Disco 2000 and the club kid scene . . . She eventually split the States altogether to study fashion in London.

As we talked she astounded me with her street smarts and dry humor, and the dizzying amount of scenes that she had been involved in by such a young age. She currently lived in the East End and worked for the fashion designer Vivienne Westwood. I felt the odd sensation that I was talking to some kind of mirror of myself, or a mirror of who I would like to be. At one point I said, "I am on an Egon Schiele kick right now," not even knowing what it meant, but it made sense to her, and I didn't feel like a fool.

I realized that maybe the reason that I could talk to her like this, without tripping myself up by being nervous or trying to impress her, was because I could look at the pair of us with a dispassionate eye and say that honestly, I felt that there was no reason why this woman would ever show an interest in me. I was a bad bet. A drug addict. Married. Unemployable. So I laid it out on the table and tried not to hide anything. It was a liberating feeling knowing that I could tell her about myself and not be afraid of rejection, because I was already rejected.

But the strangest thing happened.

She kept talking to me.

She didn't seem fazed by all of the bad stuff.

And I wondered what she saw when she looked at me.

We were oblivious as Garbage took to the stage and started playing, and the crowd at Brixton Academy began to cheer and surge to the front. It took a while before either of us even noticed the thunderous music blaring into the room. Everything had faded into the background, and we were talking about New York, and I was feeling something in my chest that I hadn't felt for a long time. I kept asking myself, "Why is she still here? Why is she still talking to me? Why is she interested? What does she see?" because her eyes did not betray any of the things that I had become accustomed to over the past few years: the suspicious look of someone who is watching a heroin addict, the pitying looks from an old friend, the superior glare of the caseworkers and doctors, the pure, terrified need of Susan. No, she was looking at me with something else in her eyes, a look and a feeling that had not been around me for so long that it momentarily felt arcane, alien, foreign.

I glanced over to the huge window that looked down onto the stage for a moment, and I realized for the first time that the band was playing, but more than that I caught a glimpse of myself reflected in the mirror, and what I saw made me jump.

Like some cheap shock effect from a bad horror movie, the reflection of what was going on in the room did not match up with my mind's perception of what should be there.

There was Vanessa, listening intently to me as I was speaking, looking momentarily confused as the words caught in my throat the moment I realized that she was talking to me.

But it was the me of seven years ago, it's true, I saw what she was seeing for a moment and it terrified and liberated me, because I looked new.

I was not broken anymore. My eyes were no longer the eyes of someone who had seen the inside of the methadone clinics and the flophouses. My arms, underneath my shirt, I instinctively knew were unscarred and unblemished, the mountain of mangled flesh and calcified veins had some-how been removed by God's hand, and they were as smooth and untouched and unruined as they were when I first came to London a lifetime ago.

And I stopped talking, struck dumb by this rev-elation.

Thinking that I was looking over to the band, she said:
"Do you want to go and see them play?"
and I answered "sure" although that was not on my mind at all
and we walked together into the crowd, making our way to the front
as the band played on
and for a moment I realized
I was reborn.

26

AFTERMATH

Coming back home could only be an ugly and depressing anticlimax. After the band was finished Vanessa had to go and so did I. Drug-need was already gnawing at the inside of me. We swapped numbers and I left. As I made my way back from Brixton to Hackney I started to feel this new excitement about my life slowly deflating from me. The streets around Murder Mile seemed as small and as cold and as lonely as ever. I slid my key into the lock and swung the metal door open, escaping from the frosty air. I walked through the concrete walkway and up the staircase leading to the flat.

When I opened the door I saw her there, nodded out on the only chair in the place, in front of a nature documentary showing animals thousands of feet underwater moving silently, and the smell of her hit me: the smell of rot, the smell of the cigarette that had burned down to her fingers and no doubt left a scorch ring on the flesh permeated everything. The flat was suddenly smaller than before. I flicked the light on, but it did not shake her out of her nod.

I walked past her and into the bathroom. The girl she was hanging out with before had obviously been here, as there were used needles on the sink of a different brand and gauge than either Susan or I used. And I hated it, but seeing the discarded needles and the dried brown blood spots on the sink, and even seeing Susan back there with all of the life evaporated out of her shell started to change me again, and undo all of the good-but-alien sensations I had been experiencing tonight. I started to realize that I was still here, I was still nothing more that a junkie idiot, that my situation was as fucked as ever. Dejectedly, I started to prepare a shot of heroin.

I heard Susan rouse from her coma.

"Hey," she croaked.

"Yeah."

I dug around, finding a new needle in the bathroom cabinet, and retrieved the bag of heroin I had hidden away from her before the tour started.

"Your friend left her old spikes here."

———

"Oh yeah. Be careful, I think she has Hep C."

"What the fuck did she leave them here for, then?"

"They're old. I gave her some of ours."

"Well, can you get rid? I don't want to touch them."

She turned the sound up on the TV again. I could hear David Attenborough's familiar voice from the other room.

"How was it?" she asked eventually.
"Fine. I met a cool girl. She was from New York."

"Oh yeah?"

It all went quiet for a moment as Susan lapsed back into the TV, and I started cooking up. The heroin fizzled in the spoon. Richard Attenborough carried on. The world was familiar and comfortable. Then Susan asked: "She use?"

"Who?"

"The girl from New York. Does she use?"

"What? Heroin?"

"Yes, heroin. What do you think I'm talking about? Caffeine?"

———

It seemed like an odd question. Susan said it as if everybody used heroin. Like it was a common defining characteristic outside of our world. I drew the dope up into the syringe and said: "I don't think so."

I tied the belt around my arm and flexed for a vein. I was going into my wrist again. My hands looked chubby and pockmarked from all of the injecting I had been doing there recently. I thought about Vanessa again. I thought about her eyes, and her lips, and the way she smelled. I thought about her outfit. I thought about her black leather boots. I thought about her voice.

"Then why the fuck," Susan asked suddenly, "was she talking to you? I mean really, what on earth could you possibly have in common?"

I ignored the question. I had already been thinking about it all of the way home. The answer was too depressing. I thought of her number, written on a piece of paper and carefully folded in my pocket. I wondered about the chance of me ever calling it, and as I fixed my shot and the heroin put me back in my place, I realized that it probably would never happen.

I cleaned myself up and tidied my stuff away. I walked back into the room. Susan was still half unconscious, her face had taken on that slack, mongoloid look people get when they are half in a nod.

———

"What the fuck are we doing here?" I asked Susan, rousing her as I walked back into the room.

"What do you mean?"

"In London. Why the fuck did we come here in the first place?"

"Because we couldn't stay in LA. What kind of stupid question is that?"
"Well, what kind of stupid reason is that to come someplace? Because you can't stay in another place? It makes no sense."

"You make no sense."

We lapsed into silence again, momentarily enjoying the drugs in our blood.

"We have no money," Susan told me eventually. "Did you get paid for the tour tonight?"

"No. I have to call Alex in the coming week. Dan has to do the accounts, and then we get paid."

"The Virgin Megastore didn't make you wait to get paid."

"That's true, Susan. You're very perceptive."

"I heard from my sister today. She had twins."

I had to scramble for the information. She talked about her sister so rarely that I almost forgot she had one.

———

"She was pregnant?"

"Yes! She was pregnant! You knew this! I told you...."
"Oh."

"Twin boys. She's going to send pictures. It must be nice. Having a family. I don't even have my own family around me anymore."

"From what you've told me that's probably a good thing."

She turned and looked at me. "Everybody needs a family. I'm thirty-five. It's almost too late for me. Do you think I could clean up in time to have a baby? I heard that you can carry a baby full term okay if you're just on methadone."

Susan talked like this every so often. It always made me slightly nauseous to hear it. She never came right out and told me that she was talking about having *my* baby, so I would let her talk about it in an abstract, theoretical way. It was okay, because I knew it would never happen. But tonight, the very idea of Susan carrying a baby around in her gut repulsed me more than usual.
"Anyone with a cunt, a working set of fallopian tubes, and a womb can have a baby," I spat. "What the fuck you are going to *do* with that baby is a different question."

She went quiet, and then said: "It would just be neat to have someone who loved me."

———

Sensing this was my cue to say something, I waited a beat and told her: "Buy a fucking cat, then."

A day passed. And then two. I didn't call Vanessa. Susan was right. What the fuck would she want with me? And the money situation dragged out. The accounts Dan had provided didn't add up and had to be redone. The record label was getting their own accountants to do the books. Expect a further delay. Susan had started doing volunteer work at a local needle exchange, but of course it was unpaid. I kept on the phone with Alex every day trying to get the money owed to me. Every day he told me that tomorrow he would definitely be able to cut a check for me.

After a week and a half, he announced that there was more work if I wanted it. A trip to Wales, to lip synch the first single on a regional television show. He promised that I would have the money before I left. Despite feeling slightly screwed over about the money situation, the chance to get out of London for even a day was too good to pass up, so I accepted.

We drove down early the next morning. The show was called *This Is It!* and was hosted by someone I vaguely remembered from a children's television show of my youth. We were to perform our song in front of an audience of twenty or so bored Welsh teenagers. We did it, and Alex finally cut our checks, handing them to us as the filming wrapped up. I was in the clear again.

———

Kelly was staying on to do press on her own, and the rest of the band was to travel back by train. We drank and walked around the studio, which was out in the middle of nowhere. Again, away from the city, I started to relax and feel freer than I had before. A film crew filmed the band drinking beers and lounging around in a games room for promotional material. The cameras gave us a sense that maybe this record was really going to happen. The whole scene was surreally out of synch with what was going on in my real life.

On the train back to London I was gripped with the familiar anxiety of returning to the flat and Susan. I opened my wallet and looked again at Vanessa's number. Ben, the guitarist, was sitting across from me listening to music. I tapped him and asked him if he had a mobile phone. He passed it over to me and plugged his earphones back in. With a sense that if I didn't do this now I never would, I dialed her number and held my breath until she picked up.

"I thought that you weren't going to call," she said to me.

"I had to call."

"Why?"

"Because things are preordained. I had to call. What are you doing?"

———

"Getting ready for a party. You want to swing by? Where are you?"

"Coming back from filming the world's cheesiest TV show. I'd love to come."

"Okay. Lets meet for drinks first. . . ."

I clicked off the phone and another phase of my life began.

27

VERSE

It seemed that as soon as I started seeing Vanessa, London started to come alive. The nights started getting shorter, the days warmer, the worries less. We met up two nights later, hit a few East End bars, and then went back to her place. We listened to music, *Loveless* by My Bloody Valentine. And then we fell into bed with all of the excitement of new lovers.

There was no nervousness. When I saw her naked for the first time all of my old feelings of sexual longing flooded back into me. It was a shocking, wonderful, electric feeling. We kissed, our tongues wrapping around each other as we fell into bed. The sex seemed to go on for hours. And when I came, I was hard again almost immediately. We fucked like horny sixteen-year-olds, discovering the opposite sex for the first time.

———

Cheshire Street, 4:00 A.M. We stagger in from a warehouse party on Brick Lane. Vanessa's breath is sharp, cutting through the still of the bedroom like glass as we have sex again. And again. And again. Her nipples are hard and I am biting at them, and I slide my cock in and out of her. Her pupils contract, locked on mine; in a flash of electric skin I reach down, rest my hands on her ass cheeks, pulling them apart, and they are slick with cum. We have been dropping pills and having sex constantly for what seems like glorious eternity. With my forefinger I rub the wetness into her asshole and withdraw my prick, repositioning, and gently ease myself into her ass instead. Her breath quickens, sharpens, then settles back into its rhythm as she reaches to her side and retrieves the vibrator, sliding it into her pussy. As I find myself all of the way in, I can feel—through my own prick—the vibrating rubber cock inside of her, parallel to my own, as we fuck ourselves into ritualized oblivion.

One afternoon, on a whim, I stop by the boutique she works at. Vanessa closes up. She takes me downstairs and shows me a dress that Courtney Love will be wearing in a few hours at some red carpet event. I dress Vanessa in it, turn her around, hitch the skirt, and slide my prick into her. Moments after we are done there is a pounding on the door, as the couriers arrive to take the dress to Courtney's hotel room. I am lost in the wonder and the glory of Vanessa's cunt. I gaze upon it, awestruck, like it is the work of a master. I feel like I am seeing a Picasso canvas, or a Dalí sculpture rendered in pure gold that has been long lost. I feel as if my eyes are the first to behold it since the moment of its creation.

Sometimes when we take Ecstasy it feels as if I can melt into it, melt into her. We become fluid and unstable, and for moments as brief as epileptic flashes, the laws of physics are suspended and we melt, tongue in cunt, cock in mouth, in a lightning crack of divinity. For moments we cease to be individuals.

"I want to do this forever," I tell her, my mouth full of her.

And sometimes there is a kind of short circuit, and I lose moments, and everything comes to me in fragments. The soft curves of her body, a hot, stiff nipple, the roundness of her ass, her endless brown eyes, the soft brown skin of her back, red hair plastered to her forehead.

My cock in her hands, her mouth, her pussy, her asshole, and it feels as if I am undergoing a religious conversion of sorts, with my mouth on her clit, crushed against her lips. I have a sense of God that I have never felt in my whole time on this earth.

Oh Christ I am in love I am in love, and it is flowing from me, I cannot stop it, and when we are lying naked, listening to music, play fighting, laughing, I never want to leave this room. This is real. Oh God help me, this is real.

28

CHORUS

After weeks of seeing Vanessa, I know that tonight I am coming as close to ruining everything as is possible. I have decided to leave Susan. I am trying to do it the best way I can. I have been spending all of my free time with Vanessa. When she is not around I am sad and withdrawn, and the only way I can cope with that is to get high. And getting high is the only hold that Susan has on me anymore.

Tonight an old Scottish junkie called Jimmy who works with Susan at the needle exchange dropped over to Murder Mile with a large quantity of pharmaceutical grade cocaine. I cannot even begin to fathom how these ampoules of liquid cocaine found their way onto the black market, but of course I cannot resist having just one shot of coke, and before I even realized where I was, it was four hours later and all of the coke was gone, and my arms were raw and bloody from at least fifty separate injections. Crashing hard from the coke, I tried to wash the blood off my arms, but my flesh looked like raw hamburger meat, so I threw on a leather jacket and split, leaving Susan and Jimmy to carry on with whatever else he had brought over with him.

By the time I arrived at Vanessa's flat, I was almost in tears from the mind-bending effects of the coke crash, and suddenly I was completely aware of the hopelessness of my situation. When I arrived, Vanessa seemed shocked at my appearance, and when I took my jacket off and she saw what I had done to my arms she was almost in tears as well. We just sat there on her bed, I rested my head on her, and she cradled me like a child until I started trying to talk to her, but everything came out as a sob. All I could say was "I'm sorry..." over and over, because I knew that there was no conceivable reason that she should have to listen to this or to put up with this from me. The beauty of what went on when we were together, the innocence of it, the carefree and joyous nature of it, was suddenly destroyed when I walked in that night. I had brought with me all of the destruction and negative energy that shaped my life, and I think that it scared her badly because for the first time she saw me as ugly, and as worn down, and as scared as I have ever been.

She kept asking me: "Do you want to go?"

And I kept saying "no" because I felt that if I went tonight, that I might never be allowed to return.

———

Vanessa has never told me that I need to stop using. It is something that has endeared her to me more than anything. Usually people find it impossible not to talk in clichés when they are around an addict, and the biggest cliché of the lot is the faux concern and the assurances that "you really need to get help." No, Vanessa in the whole time I have known her has never said any of that to me. In New York's music scene she had seen enough of addicts to understand that no one could make me quit. And sitting here on her bed, with her gently cradling my head, I realized that I had been taking advantage of her good grace and her consideration of my feelings.

How dare I walk in here with the blood not yet dried on my arms, weeping and paranoid and suicidal?

It is now that I realize that I am running out of time, and I need to make a decision. If I leave here tonight without making a decision, I may never get the opportunity to come back. So I amaze myself by being the one who first broaches the subject.

"I think I need to quit," I say. "I think that this is it. I really need to stop doing this."

Vanessa doesn't say anything for a while. Then she says: "I think you're right."

We sit there. I can feel some of the horror receding a little. I have done this many times. I know the stages of the cocaine crash. It will be a while before I feel anything close to normal, and as the cocaine wears off I start to feel the pain in my arms and hands from the repeated, frenzied injecting I had been doing earlier in the night.

"I don't want to go back there," I say eventually.

"Where?"

"The flat. I have to tell Susan. I have to do it now."

We lapse back into silence for a while.

"Would you like to stay here?" Vanessa asks, eventually.

"Yes. Are you inviting me to move in with you?"

"Yes. But were you serious about stopping doing this?"

"Yes."

There is of course a huge fear about leaving Susan and moving in with Vanessa. In fact, Susan and Vanessa are almost side players to the real drama that was unfolding in my head. If I move in with Vanessa, one of two things will have to happen: either I would have to get clean or Vanessa would have to start using heroin. The situation could not resolve any other way. So my choice is not between Susan and Vanessa, which would really be no choice at all. My choice is between the status quo of my existence as it is or an attempt to live another kind of life.

29

COMING IN TO LAND

Walking from Murder Mile with a bag of my clothes in a holdall, I stop to call Vanessa from a pay phone.

"It's me," I tell her. "Is it cool to come over?"

"Sure. What's going on?"

"I left Susan. It's done."

"What happened?"

"I don't want to talk about it. Maybe later, but not now."

It is curious, because the relationship that I have had with Susan would be unfathomable to Vanessa—indeed, sometimes it is unfathomable to even me—and I feel like I am talking in riddles when I try to explain it. I have been through break-ups before. Some extremely messy, some pro-tracted, but none as oddly noneventful as this one.

I started the conversation by telling Susan that Vanessa and I had been sleeping together. I had spent most nights over at her place since that first time. I expected that she already had assumed this, and Susan seemed entirely nonplussed by the information. She said something along the lines of "Well, if that's what you need to do."
"It is what I need to do."

"Well, fine. What are you telling me for? Is this supposed to turn me on?"

We lapsed into silence again. I had waited until Susan was high on dope, because I had seen her completely break down about the smallest thing—from a phone call from her father to a charity appeal on television—if she wasn't suffi-ciently insulated from reality with drugs. But so far, so good.

"I am telling you, because I am going to move in with her. I think we have a future together, and I don't think that you and I have a future to-gether."

Susan lit a cigarette, and I noticed her hands were shaking. I was struck again by how much like a little old lady she was beginning to look. Her eyes betrayed fear, despite the opiates in her. She sucked in a lungful of smoke.

———

"What about my paperwork? I'm illegal here. You're abandoning me and now I will never be legal here."

"You won't be legal even if I stay. We didn't even begin to file your papers in the whole time that we've been here."

"But what am I going to do?"

I could hear that old hysterical note creeping into her voice. This was it. I had to do it now.
"I can't help you anymore. My life doesn't lie here. You knew this wouldn't last. We never got married thinking that we would grow old together. I've found something else I want."

There was silence again.

"Then go," she said, quietly. "Just go."

And that was it. No tears, no screaming, no begging to stay. I packed my things and walked out. What do you do, when you make a suicide pact but both of you survive? Was I a coward for not trying again?

As I walked toward the train station, I realized for the first time in years I was walking with purpose. I walked Murder Mile, past the Jamaican patty stand, and the fried chicken and halal kebab signs, past the junk shops and the kids lurking by the pay phones hawking crack and stolen mobile phones. I felt my chest loosening, as if I were really breathing for the first time in

years. I walked into the sodium glow and train
rumble of Clapton station and I realized that
for the first time in recent memory I was not
afraid.

30

THE GOOD TIMES

We are in a warehouse party in Hackney. An old band mate from Los Angeles was in town doing the lighting for a Black Rebel Motorcycle Club show with the Libertines headlining. He called me out of the blue to tell me he was in town.

Vanessa and I walk in there around midnight on the tail end of a forty-eight-hour cocaine, Ecstasy, and sex bender that has taken us to a variety of bars, clubs, flats, and houses all over the city. As we stagger into the place, all eyes turn to us. We are on fire, radiating an aura of invincibility that everybody is picking up on. A man walks up to us and asks, "Can I take your photo?" and we say yes, so he does, temporarily blinding us with the flash. He hands us his card and says, "E-mail me and I will send you the picture!" and we walk away as if it were the most natural thing in the world.

——

The DJ is spinning Primal Scream at a thunderous volume, and we dance and kiss to "Swastika Eyes" furiously. Love and empathy is radiating out from us in great telepathic waves. I am swimming in Vanessa's eyes, lost in them for a moment.

Somebody bumps into me, and it is the guy from the Libertines, Pete Doherty, and he looks as if he is about to collapse onto the floor. His skin is ashen, and he is barely standing really, his eyes fuzzy and unfocussed.

"Sorry mate," he slurs, rocking on unsteady heels.

"No problem."

And then he staggers away, careening into someone else.

"He's gonna play tonight?" Vanessa laughs. "He looks like he won't make it."

A guy comes onstage and is joined by a DJ, who starts to blast abrasive metallic noise. The singer, a tall, spastic-looking skinhead, obviously half-deranged on Ecstasy, starts to rap over the top of the music in lunatic yelps. The place is suddenly packed, shoulder to shoulder, and we are drawn toward the front of the stage by the swell of people and the heat is brutal and the noise is almost terrifying and it feels like we are at the end of the world and my eyes catch Vanessa's and I never want this to stop, never never want it to stop.

Spilling out into the night air. The Ecstasy has come on so strong we both looked at each other at the same time as Black Rebel Motorcycle played and we decided—without speaking—"Home. Bed," because we could no longer be contained by clothes.

And in the taxi home I rest my head on her lap and look up at her face as the streetlights bounce from her cheeks and I say: "My God. The scene is so incredible right now. . . . It feels as if there is fucking revolution in the air. . . . When did London wake up all of a sudden?"

And Vanessa laughs, telling me: "London wasn't asleep. You were."

She is right, of course. And we laugh, as the taxi speeds us home so we can fuck frenziedly until the sun rises again.

Shoreditch. The weekend of the Queen's Golden Jubilee, and all of London it seems is staggering from one party to another, blissfully drunk and wasted. Wherever you go, carefree hedonism is the order of the day. The days are endless, warm, and infused with the surreal logic of dreams. We are drinking beers and people-watching from a sun-drunk table outside of the Barley Mow, enjoying the bustle of Curtain Road. It seems as if the whole population of the city is emerging into the light for the first time, blinking molelike into the mid-morning sun.

"Do you know something?" I tell her.

"What?"

"It's been three months since we met."

She laughs.

"I have something for you."
She smiles and looks over. I reach into my pocket and take out one of my old AA sobriety chips. It is red, and on one side is inscribed "90 DAYS" and on the other "ONE DAY AT A TIME." She looks at it and smiles. I smile too.

"This is so cool," she says. "Thank you!"

She places it on her key ring, and we pick up our beers, clanking them together.

"One day at a time," we toast, as we drink. Vanessa is so beautiful today. She makes the sun on my face feel warmer. She makes the beer I am drinking seem colder. We are free.

31

THE BAD TIMES

After moving into Vanessa's bedroom in Cheshire Street for a month or so, we decided to get our own place. She shared her old place with a few girls who seemed slightly annoyed by an uninvited lodger showing up and holding up the line to the communal shower. We found a decrepit artist loft above a fried chicken joint on Kingsland Road, so I changed my pickup to a new pharmacy, ten minutes down the road. The pharmacy sat on a nondescript row of shops, surrounded by a video store and a Greek bakery. The old woman behind the counter regarded me sourly but did not treat me too badly.

The loft in Dalston was an unmitigated disaster. Upon moving in we had discovered that it was infested with mice and cockroaches. Also, the electricity did not work properly and most nights the place felt like a walk-in refrigerator. When we complained to the landlord he claimed that since the place was technically a commercial property and not a residential one, he did not have to do a thing about it.

To compound the problem, a month after we moved in, Vanessa discovered that she was pregnant. We had stopped using protection after we moved in together. Our connection was so immediate and so profound that I thought nothing of doing this. One week her period was late, so she bought a home test from the pharmacy and the results came back positive. My first reaction was complete terror. I assumed that Vanessa's would be the same. But when she saw my face turn white she seemed hurt.

"Is this really such a bad thing?" she asked. "I mean, if this was such a bad thing why didn't we take precautions?"

I thought about it. Was it a bad thing? I had never even entertained the thought of children before. But I had never entertained the thought of quitting dope before either. I looked at Vanessa and realized that maybe we did have a chance to make it in this world. Maybe it was time to take risks and think the unthinkable.
"No." I said finally, "Not such a bad thing at all."

The band's activity following the TV show in Wales ground to a halt. The release date on the album was put back. The single from the album was decided upon and changed at least a dozen times. Throughout all of this, Alex proved himself to be possibly the most ineffectual manager of all time.

The check from the Garbage tour bounced, and I took a job working in a music shop in the West End to supplement my income. I was on the phone to Alex begging him and then demanding that he pay me my money so often that he started screening my calls. What kept me going was the idea that soon the call would come to announce that our album was being released and that we could go back on the road. Only the call never came. Other calls came. The news that a DJ had been paid fifteen thousand pounds to remix the single, and soon after that the song had been dropped from the album altogether. The news that the A&R guy representing the band had been fired and replaced by someone who thought that our album sounded "outdated." The news that our European label was suing our UK label over the lack of activity. The final straw came over an argument about underarm hair.

A new single was decided upon, and a video was shot with Kelly to promote it. The song stank. The label demanded that Kelly record a poppier-sounding single to launch the album with and she did, without the band knowing. The first I heard of it was when a CD of the song landed in my mailbox. It sounded insipid, desperate. Of course, the label loved it. Despite not finding their way to pay me the money they still owed me for rehearsals, and for the Garbage tour that had happened almost a year previously, they suddenly

found fifty thousand pounds to shoot a new promotional video.

All was apparently going well. Until the day when
I spoke to Kelly over the phone to find out the
state of play, and she told me the latest piece of
shitty luck to befall the project.

"The single isn't being released," she said.

"What? Why?"

"Well, when the label saw the finished product
they freaked because in two of the shots I raised
my arms and they could see underarm hair."

I sat down.

"The exact word they used was *disgusting*. Can
you believe that?"

"That's crazy."

"They wanted to reshoot the video, but I said no.
There've been too many delays already."

"Right."

"And I told them Patti Smith had underarm hair.
It didn't ruin her career!"

"Right. And Nena."

"Nena?"

———

"Yeah, '99 Red Balloons,' remember?"

"Oh yeah."

"So what happened?"

"Well, they went behind my back and spent fifteen grand digitally touching up the video to remove the hair."

"Jesus Christ."

"I know. I freaked when Alex told me. So I told the label that I would not promote the single or the album unless they put the underarm hair back in."

"And what did they say?"

"They're threatening to sue me. But I have to stick to my guns, don't you think?"

The flat was particularly cold that day. I detected some movement from the corner of my eye, and saw a monstrous cockroach making a break across the kitchen floor.

Vanessa was at work, and there wasn't enough food in the fridge to eat.

"Oh yeah," I told her, "you have to stick to your guns."

Sickened and disappointed, I walked to the newsagent to pick up a copy of *NME*. When I picked up the new issue, a familiar face was staring back at me from the front cover. It was Elektra's

husband, Tom, with a big smug grin on his face.
The headline read: "The Ones: Say Hello to Your
New Favorite Band!" I put the paper back in dis-
gust and stormed out into the filth and chaos of
Dalston High Street.

Vanessa started bleeding the following Friday
night, and by Saturday evening the pain in her
belly was so bad that we were in the emergency
room at 10:00 P.M. with the first round of the
East End's weekend casualties. Red-faced drunks
nursing broken noses and picking chunks of glass
out of their mangled faces. Old women who didn't
have the sense to just die before they hit seventy,
silently fretting about strokes or heart attacks.
Screaming infants with tired, worried-looking
parents.

The doctors rushed Vanessa in to a cold little
examining room, lifted her shirt, probed her
belly with latex-clad hands, and announced that
she was miscarrying and there was nothing to
do but wait it out. Since the pregnancy was in the
first trimester it would, as the doctor said, make
its own way out without need for medical intervention. They sent us home with a prescription
for codeine and a couple of leaflets about dealing
with the loss of an unborn child.

The flat in Dalston seemed more empty and colder
than ever. We walked in and I heard the frenzied
squealing of a mouse stuck to one of the glue traps
we left around the place. The doctor told us that
there was no specific reason why we lost the baby,
and that many pregnancies ended in miscarriage

this early on. So with no one else to blame, I took it out on the mouse. I smashed its skull in with a ball hammer, ending its life with a little more venom than usual. Tonight the blood seemed almost too red, counterfeit, like something from a joke shop. The skin held together, the shape of its head elongated, and crimson poured from its mouth as it kicked spastically with a back leg, before becoming still. I threw it out in the bins around the back, still stuck to the trap.

We sat on the edge of the bed in silence. I wanted to cry, but I stopped myself. Somehow, Vanessa wasn't crying and I couldn't bear it if she did. If I cried, then we would both have to cry and that would be the worst thing in the world that could happen. I looked at the box of codeine that the doctors had prescribed. They were over-the-counter strength—eight milligrams codeine to five hundred milligrams paracetamol. Vanessa groaned and held her stomach.

"How bad does it feel?"

"Horrible. I can feel my stomach contracting. It's the most horrible feeling."
"Fucking assholes," I hissed, throwing the box of codeine on the floor. "This shite wouldn't shift a fucking toothache. Do you want something that's going to take the pain away for real?"

Vanessa nodded silently. I rummaged around in my pockets and produced a wrap of heroin. In all the time we had been together she had never so much as expressed an interest in trying smack. In the club scenes of New York she had seen heroin so often that I suppose my lifestyle was not particularly shocking to her. She had never had a drug problem in the sense that I had a drug problem, so I felt somewhat reassured about giving her some under these circumstances. I placed a small amount of it on aluminum foil and showed her how to smoke it.

We had almost bought a crib last week from the Egyptian man who had helped us move from Cheshire Street. All I could think was how relieved I was that we hadn't bought it. I imaged us both, sitting in this roach and mouse-infested hole, smoking heroin, waiting for Vanessa to finish miscarrying with an empty crib in the middle of it all like an accusing finger. Maybe that would have been the final straw.

Vanessa smoked a little. It eased her pain. I injected a little and it eased mine also. I said to her: "We could always try again, you know."

"I know."
"Maybe it would be better this way. We'd be prepared for the baby instead of just dealing with it because it happened."

"I suppose."

We smoked more, silently. There was nothing more to say. Vanessa went back to the bathroom, the blood kept coming, and so did the pain.

———

In three days the bleeding stopped, and Vanessa stopped smoking heroin. Her self-control astounded me. She seemed utterly disinterested in the drug and its effects, beyond its usefulness as a pain reliever. She was some kind of miracle, I thought. When we started having sex again, we did not use protection. Having a child snatched away from us had awakened something in us that we couldn't quite articulate. It felt as if something were wrong in the universe, and it was our job to put it right. That the loss of the child was not what was meant to happen. This child was meant to be born, was meant to be in this world, was meant to have us as its parents.

Three weeks after the miscarriage we found out that, again, Vanessa was pregnant. She made an appointment with her GP and he confirmed what the home test had told us. We were going to be parents.

32

ON THE STREET

In the end I left the custody of Dr. Ira without any
of the fireworks that I had imagined. He did not
die on the end of a blade wielded by me or burn up
in a guzzling fire that I started in the clinic. No,
I simply walked out of the hospital one day and
never came back.

I had no intentions of doing it that day.

We had fled Dalston for a one-bedroom flat in
Stamford Hill. Since the landlord had refused
to fix up the place, we stopped paying rent, fitted
the doors with padlocks, and started looking for
a new place to live. We used the withheld rent to
put the down payment on the new flat.

I was heading down to the pharmacy to get my
methadone and then I was due to sign the lease

and pick up the keys for the new place that same afternoon. Lingering by a pay phone on the edges of a housing estate was a tall, thin woman whose dirty-blond hair fell about her face in filthy clumps.

"You got some change?" she asked, pulling on a cigarette with shaking hands and looking at me pleadingly. Her skin was pitted and scarred with acne. She had a trace of a Scottish accent and wore only a thin white T-shirt and jeans, despite the brutal cold. I handed her some coins, scraped out of my pocket.

"Aw shit, thanks," she said. "I need to make a call. I've been up all night."

"Oh yeah?"

"Yeah. It's been a long one." She twitched slightly. "This is shit, isn't it?"

"Yes, it is," I told her before carrying on to get my methadone.

I walked toward the pharmacy. Approaching the street I noticed POLICE LINE—DO NOT CROSS tape blocking my way. The traffic had been building steadily as I approached and I soon realized why. Police directed traffic away from the street, and drivers sat nullified by frustration or cursed silently behind rolled-up windows. I approached the nearest cop, a sour-faced woman with gray skin and dead, light-blue eyes, and asked what was happening.

———

"Gas leak," she replied, with a voice like shaved glass. "The street's been sealed off."

"But I need to get to the chemist's over there."

"Closed. It's all closed. There's another chemist back up that way on Dalston High Street."

"I need to go to this chemist."

"It's closed. Gas leak."

I walked back to the housing estate where I had seen the woman. She was long gone. A fish and chips shop on the edge of the estate was opening up for the day. I called the clinic and got through on the second ring.

"Homerton DDU."
"I need to speak to Dr. Ira. I'm one of his clients."

"He's busy. Is this because of the gas leak by any chance?"

"Yeah."

"We're doing an emergency dispensing service at the clinic. Come in and we'll take care of it."

"I can't come in. I have a really important appointment in an hour. Can't I go to another chemist?"

"No. You have to come in."

———

"Then I'll have to do without today. I can't come in."

"Wait a minute."

They placed me on hold. I found myself listening to Musak momentarily. Kenny G plays the hits of Celine Dion. I wondered if that would be playing when I die. The phone box stank of stale döner kebabs and vomit.

"Hello?"

"Yes."

"I just spoke to Dr. Ira. He said that if you miss a dose it will be considered an infraction and you will be placed back on a supervised consumption program until your case can be reevaluated."

"Can I speak to Dr. Ira please?"

"Dr. Ira is busy. We close at four o'clock. See you soon."

I hung up the phone. They had me. Again they had me. Cursing, I headed toward the tube.

In the waiting room junkies sprawled on chairs and squatted against the wall and coughed and spat phlegm into Kleenexes, watching the clock agitatedly. I took my number and waited. Within minutes one of the male nurses appeared and called my name. Surprised, I walked over.

"That was quick," I said. "You have a full house today."

"Well this is just for your urine test."

"Urine test?"

"Yup. You don't have a problem with that, do you?"

"Oh no. Not me."

Bastards.

Since Vanessa fell pregnant we had stopped partying altogether, but this weekend I had cracked and scored a bag of heroin from RJ. I knew that Dr. Ira would think it was his fucking birthday when my urine lit up the test like a fucking Christmas tree. I would be back on supervised consumption for months.

There was no way out. I considered pretending that I couldn't piss as I stood, dick in hand, staring at the little bottle that was about to ruin my life. The nurse waited behind me, the cubicle door open so he could observe. Then, deciding against any more delays, I filled the bottle up with heroin-laced piss and handed it to the nurse.

"Thanks," he said. "You can wait outside."

I could feel the old fear and helplessness rising in me. I needed to get out of the methadone clinics. They were killing me. This was no way to live.

Again I was having to keep my change of address a secret for fear of being stuck at yet another clinic as a newcomer, with an even more uncaring and fucked-up prescribing regime than Dr. Ira's. It was perfectly obvious that while I remained addicted to state-mandated opiates, I was no longer in control of my own destiny. Every decision I made would have to be approved by a room full of shit-eating soulless fucks like Dr. Ira. I was a helpless fucking pawn. A laboratory rat. I was worth less than the shit on the sole of Dr. Ira's boot.

I looked at my watch. It was thirty minutes before I was due to meet with my new landlord to sign the lease. If I walked out right now I would be cutting it fine. But they hadn't even called me yet. There still seemed to be at least a dozen junkies ahead of me waiting to get dosed. I pulled out my mobile phone and frantically started to dial the landlord's number.

Out of nowhere I found myself grabbed by the collar and spun around. I was looking into the twisted face of one of the slack-jawed security guards they sometimes had on duty in this place. They all wore these terrible-looking polyester uniforms, and all had the same kind of lobotomized look about their faces. This one could have been no more than twenty and spoke with an almost incomprehensible West Indian patois.

"Geddafuck out wi'da phone!" he yelled at me.

"What?"

———

"No phone! Geddafuckout wi'da phone, man!"

He pointed to a sign on the wall, an illustration of a mobile phone with a red line through it. Normally I would have apologized to this prick and left the clinic to make the call, but, finally, today, I had had my limit of what I was taking.

"Get your fucking hands off me," I warned him.

"Shutup man! Don' talk smart, boy! Now geddafuck out, yeah?"

Suddenly we were the center of attention. I snarled and pressed my face close to his.
"Why don't you go fuck yourself! If you don't get your fucking hand off my collar, this phone is going right up your useless fucking asshole!"

I landed on the concrete outside with a thud. The security guard brushed himself off and stood there, looking down on me. He laughed, "Dickhead!" before spitting and walking back into the clinic. I got up, brushed myself off, and started to walk away. As I walked past a pay phone I lifted the receiver and smashed it back down with a crunch, cracking the plastic open. Walking back I called Vanessa, who could sense by the hysterical tone of my voice that something had happened.

"I'm done," I told her. "I'm out of the clinics. I'm finished."
"Really?"

———

"Really. That's it. I got to find a doctor who will detox me, and then I'm done."

"Are you sure?"

"Believe me," I said, glancing back toward the hospital that had caused me so much humiliation and pain in the past, "I'm fucking sure."

33

DR. CASH

Ugh.
Clean again.

The lie at the heart of treatment centers, the recovery industry, and self-help groups is that life off drugs is any better than life on them. A preposterous idea. The two states coexist in a parallel sense—to say that one is preferable to the other is to miss the point entirely.

And here I was—clean again. I could pass a urine test. If a car hit me, the meager amounts of morphine the hospital would allow me would actually work to ease my suffering. I could buy a ticket, step on a plane, and go anywhere I liked. But sitting in the doctor's office, with my head in my hands, I wondered what the sense in that could be. If there were no drugs waiting for me at the other side, why would I even bother making the trip?

Since coming off opiates I felt that I was hanging on to my sanity with slipping fingers. I was gripped by murderous rages and bouts of severe, suicidal depression. Riding the underground: the rush of the stale air pushed through ancient black tunnels—without drugs in my blood the ugliness and venality of humanity exposed in all of its sickening glory—the scum and the human flotsam floated by, thoughtlessly consuming my oxygen.

On the platform, an obnoxious bastard in a business suit blocked my way as I rushed to make the train. As I approached, he sneezed a wet, theatrical sneeze right in my face without covering his mouth—spraying me with moisture—and I froze, momentarily stunned, before lashing out at the fucking pig's head with my fist—*thud!*— connecting only with the train's door as it slid shut, separating us. The cunt just stared at me with a sardonic grin, mouthing "Fuck you, mate" through the window, and the rage, uncontrollable and building in me like an atomic flash—screaming incoherent red-faced manias at him—startled commuters starting to give me a wide berth— GETOUTHEREYOUDISTGUSTINGFAT FUCKI'LLCUTYOURFUCKINGTHROAT YAFUCKIN'CUNT—the engine revving and the train slowly—PIECEOFSHITI'LLDROWN YOUINYOUROWNFUCKIN'BLOOD— pulling out of the station and the gloating bastard is allowing himself a smirk as I trot after the

train for a—FAGGOTCOCKSUCKING-
CHICKENSHITBASTARD—moment, halfheartedly punching the door again *BAM* again
BAM again *BAM*—CUUUUNT!—and the fucker
actually smirks and flicks the V's before disappear-
ing off, off into the murky underground gloom.

In his office, Dr. Cash is polite and respectful as
always. He has the airbrushed look of an American newscaster, a Madame Tussauds waxwork
figure, or a presidential candidate. He is flushed
and pink with good living. Private doctors are a
different breed from the types you find yourself
stuck with on the NHS when you are a junkie.
If I could only afford it, I would remain under
the care of croakers like Cash for the rest of my
long, strung-out life. Unfortunately, I have to
reserve my use of the good doctor for occasions
like this—detoxification. I found Dr. Cash on
the junkie grapevine. He prescribed injectable
methadone to an old junkie I occasionally bought
off and was one of the few private doctors in the
city who was still willing to take on new clients
after the government started cracking down on
such practices.

"So, how have you been feeling?"

"Insane."

"Hmmm." Cash flicked through his file with long,
delicate fingers. "And you've been opiate-free for
two weeks now, is that correct?"

"Yes."

———

"How are you sleeping?"

"Shitty."

"Well, getting sleep is important. Does the Valium help?"

"A little."

"Well, we'll up your dose a little. And what else? You said 'insane.' Depressed?"

"Depressed. Angry. Ready to kill."

"Well, an adjustment phase is to be expected. . . ." The detox had taken a month to fully complete. My methadone was reduced until I was taking only twenty milliliters daily. Then I stopped taking methadone for twenty-four hours. After that I switched to a drug called Subutex, which came in the form of white tablets that dissolved under the tongue. Of course, I tried to crush them up and snort them, but the rush was weak, and snorting crushed Subutex felt like snorting a large pile of flour. The Subutex was reduced until I was taking only 0.1 milligrams per day and then I stopped altogether, switching to Valium and marijuana. The physical withdrawal was something I could deal with. But the mental effects were destroying me.

"I dunno, Dr. Cash. I've been here before. . . . Hoped it might be different this time. . . . I'm starting to think that I can't cope with life. You know . . . life without smack."

––––

"Well . . . certain scientific journals have suggested that the damage from long-term opiate use is—in some cases—irreversible."

"I can't face a lifetime on methadone anymore, Dr. Cash. It's wearing me down. I'm tired."

"It doesn't have to be methadone. I mean, I can't write you a prescription for heroin without a license . . . and since the black wind of prohibition blew over from the other side of the Atlantic those licenses are not realistically obtainable anymore . . . most of the doctors who have them are old, dying off, and not in the market for taking on new patients. But I have known you for a while now, and I can see that you're on the level. A morphine maintenance program would certainly not be out of the question."

"It isn't the methadone itself, doctor—it's the clinics. Anyway, I can't afford a private maintenance program. This detox has nearly wiped me out."

I didn't look to Cash for any kind of sympathetic response because I knew instinctively that there would be none. Private doctors aren't there to take on charity cases any more than heroin dealers are. Their universe is quantitative and the prices are fixed.

"I mean if they'd just put a fucking tap outside the clinic where we could just fucking line up and get the shit dispensed every day I'd stay on methadone until I dropped dead. It's the rest of the bullshit that comes with treatment—the amateur-hour pop psychology, the constant supervision, and the encroachment on your time. The real problem is that keeping up a methadone habit is just as much work as keeping up a heroin habit. When I started doing this I never imagined I would find myself pissing in bottles every week and stuck with compulsory meetings with failed shrinks for the rest of my life. There's just no joy in this anymore."

I walked out of there carrying the handwritten prescription like I was holding a one-hundred-pound note. Nothing to do but keep on going. Dr. Cash faded out as I hit the gray streets and the evening-time cold shocked me out of the dreamy state his warm office had lulled me into.

34

CLEAN

The next day I opened my eyes.

Fuck.

The fear was on me already, sitting heavy and dark on my sallow chest. My throat felt swollen, painful. This was a new symptom. The beginnings of a cold or maybe the flu. I thought absently of the cocksucker who sneezed on me the day before on the northern line and cursed silently.

Vanessa was in the bathroom, getting ready to go to work. She had been a rock to me throughout this. We did not have an easy time in the weeks since I quit Subutex. When she returned from work I would usually be perched on the sofa, smoking a joint, on the verge of or in tears. I kept promising her that this would be over soon.

Every morning I woke up with a dread feeling in my soul.

She stood there, impossibly beautiful in the bedroom doorway. She was smiling. I managed a weak smile back at her.

"Will you be okay today?"

"Yeah. Thanks, baby. I'll be okay."

"Well, I got to go. I'm late again. I'll call you, okay?"

"Okay."

I looked at the clock: 8:30 A.M. The day stretched out in front of me, daunting and infinite. How to fill the time before I could retreat back into our bed, swallow Valium, and be unconscious again? My muscles ached and my sinuses hurt. Motherfucker. My first cold in years.

Heroin somehow prevents the body from contracting colds and the flu. You'll never see a junkie with a cold, unless of course he is in withdrawal. Once the heroin is removed, though, the weakened immune system is particularly susceptible to colds and other viruses. I coughed and sat up. I realized that I had two options: score some heroin or get out of the flat and pass the next twelve hours any way I could.

Later, I was wandering the Warren Street tube station with my hand buried in my jacket pocket, clutching a small knife. The blade was retracted, and I was scanning the blank crowd for the correct face. *The bastard must be around here: he was rushing to meet the train yesterday afternoon. He must work close by. Maybe I've already missed him.* I knew somewhere in the back of my mind that what I was doing was patently ridiculous. But I carried on, grimly determined.

I did not aim to kill or even seriously injure him. Just slash the germ-spreading bastard a little. The leg, the buttock, somewhere painful but not dangerous. I pictured the scene as I stalked the platform: there the bastard would be, rushing, late for the office. . . . I'd shadow him off the platform and as he stepped onto the escalator I'd quickly sink the blade into his soft, fat, useless ass cheek, vanishing before the pain even hit . . . before the red started to soak through the seat of his pants.

But the faces that surrounded me—beaten down, rushing, furrowed in concentration, laughing, frowning—simply exhausted me. I could feel the heat rising off my body. My legs felt weak and shaky.

"This is ludicrous," a voice told me. "You are out of your fucking mind."

Finally I sat on the platform and rested my head in my hands. My mind was screaming like some endless horror movie jump cut. It is at this point in the withdrawal process—when the smack is almost all out of your system—that the brain makes its final all-out attempt to get drugs. It wants junk. It *needs* it. It pleads and begs and cajoles. And sitting alone on a train platform having just spent an hour trying to find a man who sneezed on me yesterday so I could take revenge by stabbing him in the ass, I began to concede. Why was I even bothering to go through with this charade? I could be at Kings Cross in fifteen minutes and high within thirty.

On the next bench sat two drunken Australians drinking lager and eating like pigs from a greasy Burger King bag. The smell of the food and their whining accents was making me feel sicker than I already was. They noticed me bristle in discomfort.

"Oi mate," one yelled over to me. "Cheer up—it might never happen! Argh! Ha ha ha!"

The guy who yelled—a red-faced inbred in a U2 T-shirt—cracked up at his own witticism. I did not dignify him with a response. The train was due to arrive in four minutes, and I would soon be on my way to some heroin, which—even though it will be of mediocre quality at best—would still transform my day from the wreck it was right now.

"He don't wanna talk to you, mate," his friend chimed in, a pig-fucking retard with a grimy, sweaty-looking beard. "Strong silent type, eh?"

I gripped the knife in my pocket, blood-red murderous rage building in my chest. They had no idea how close they were to dying. I kept looking at my feet, focusing my thoughts on getting on the next train and getting the fuck out of there. No distractions.

Then the platform's PA system buzzed into life to announce that "due to a person under a train at Kings Cross," trains would no longer be stopping at this station. All around me people cursed, sighed in frustration, and stomped away to alternate platforms. Consumed by hopelessness, I finally relented. Submitting, I let my head fall into my hands, and I began to sob quietly.

35

JUNKYARD ZEN

Saturday. Vanessa was at work, and I was sitting in the house contemplating suicide. It sounds dramatic, but there it is. Vanessa's belly was showing a nice little bump now, and I was trying to be normal. Trying and failing. I woke up and I smoked weed, hoping that somewhere in that unpleasant, disorienting high I would at least get relief from the screaming in my head. Nothing. I was going to be a father soon. I sat in the chair and stared out the window. A father. Me?

The phone rang. It was Vanessa. She had taken to calling me every few hours to see if I was okay. She was the pregnant one, yet she felt she had to check on me to make sure I was all right. Some father I was going to be. Her sympathy had a curious dual effect on me: my heart skipped to hear her voice and to know that for now she still loved me and was tolerating me through my withdrawal. But when I put the phone down, like the crash from smoking crack, the depression kicked in worse than ever.

You're meant to be the strong one. She's fucking pregnant! Where are your fucking balls?

I tried to cry but there was nothing. I almost considered going through my pockets again, to try and find a bag of heroin or some methadone tablets I may have forgotten about and missed the last time I searched my pockets. It was nothing more than a trick to distract myself for the twenty minutes or so it would take to do it. But I didn't have the energy. I thought about cutting my wrists, but my muscles ached so much I could not even imagine walking over to the kitchen counter to pick up a knife. And then, Jesus, if I am going to cut my wrists, why not just score heroin instead?

My mind circled itself in this maddening dance of despair every moment of the day.

I fled the house and rode the train to the West End, wandering the streets of Soho, eventually finding myself walking along junk lines and in the shadow of the Centre Point building. There I see Imtiaz Ali, an old twisted-up Pakistani junkie I recognized from the methadone clinic. He wore a skullcap and a filthy-looking patch over his left eye, and was huddled over in the mid-morning chill; when he met my gaze, he smiled and beckoned me over.

———

"I don't see you anymore!" He laughed. "Did you move?"

"No. . . . I quit."

"Quit?"

Imtiaz laughed, and his laugh turned into a coughing fit that racked his entire body. He spat out a mouthful of phlegm and wiped his mouth with the back of his hand.
"You quit! That's very good, my friend. I wish you the best with it."

I had once heard through Steve Cook, who knew the story of every junkie in East London it seemed, that Imtiaz had lost his eye up in Bradford when crack dealers had beat him to within an inch of his life over some failed rip-off or other. Ever resourceful, Imtiaz used the missing eye as a prop to hustle money at mosques the length and breadth of London. Going through his routine of the fellow Muslim who had fallen on hard times, he would spin fictitious tales of his life spent in the service of Islam, and resisting Western infidels at every turn. Then, for the coup de grace, he would lean in to his victim and hiss, *"You see . . . this eye . . . ?"* before dramatically flipping up the dirty eye patch, revealing the grisly void underneath. *"Gouged out by a Russian bayonet while resisting the Godless communists in Afghanistan!"*

Of course, the nearest Imtiaz had gotten to Afghanistan was the Afghan heroin he injected daily . . . and right on schedule, he was waiting for his connection to show. He saw the hesitation and hunger in my eyes when he told me this.

"I think I'd better go," I said, with little conviction. I looked toward the underground station but remained rooted to the spot. Imtiaz eyed me with junkie indifference. Then he shot me a grin and said: "He's had great rock recently. Good brown, too. It's up to you, mate . . . but, well . . . one hit never put anyone back on, did it?"

I sat on the toilet in the Burger King on Tottenham Court Road and measured out some of the heroin into a bottle cap. Then I added a packet of citric acid. Placing the cap on the sink, I snapped off a healthy chunk of the rock and dropped it into the spoon, added a little water, and started to cook the solution down. The water fizzled, turned a murky brown color. The smell of the cocaine and the heroin filled the bathroom. I swirled the solution to check for residue. Hardly any. I dropped a tiny ball of toilet paper into the liquid and filtered the shot into an orange-top insulin needle bought from Imtiaz for a pound.

"I am a man of weak will," I told myself, as I slid the needle into my wrist. Painful, but those veins were the ones that had always come through for me. Typically I was quite careless with the needle, sticking it through the skin and then probing violently underneath until I found a vein. Push all the way to the hilt—nothing. Retract slightly, change the angle—push.

All the way to the hilt—nothing. Retract, change the angle, push all the way—

_____

SHIT!

Jangling pain as the needle jabs a nerve ending, sending a jolt of electricity up my left arm and one of my fingers starts tingling violently with pins and needles. FUCK!

Nothing. Retract slightly. Change the angle.

Push.

And then something. I felt it before I saw it, that junkie sixth sense. I knew I was close and then—

Pop!

The needle was in the vein and my blood was flowing, siphoned into the barrel of the syringe. Got you, you fucking bastard! I loosened the tourniquet and emptied the barrel into my aching wrist.

The whole bathroom pulsated with the intensity of the cocaine I'd injected. My head spun momentarily. My mouth felt as if it had been stuffed with wads of cotton. I could hear voices reverberating from the next room through the tiled walls. Everything sounded fuzzy and indistinct.

Everything tightened up, fell back into place. I felt alive again. I had to pack up my equipment and get out of the bathroom. Too confined. Too much bad energy. I wondered how many junkies had shot up on this toilet seat.

———

Fuck.

Fuck.

Head is ringing.

Too confined, but where to go? Not the street. The noises! The people—the shapes—the movement—too much! I am acutely oversensitive right now. Fuck, I wish I were at home. I hate doing coke in public. Fuck! I shouldn't have done this. I was surely almost over the worst of the withdrawal by now. Will this put me back? I have to tell Vanessa. Will Vanessa leave me? Will she understand?

I staggered out the door. Out onto the streets. Sensory overload. Cut across Tottenham Court Road heading for the underground. A car horn comes on like a shotgun blast.
BLAM
Jump cut—
The hood of the car inches away from me—black guy behind the wheel screaming obscenities silently through the windshield.

"Fuck! Sorry!" he is saying.

No wait—
"Fuck sorry," I am saying, staggering across the road and onto the pavement. Cold. My breath hangs suspended in the air momentarily, then it's gone into the cosmos. I start to think about something Vanessa told me once about these things called fractals. But it's too much—too crazy right now!

———

I feel like a monster, something that should be living deep, deep underground rather than up here in the unforgiving glare of the winter sun. The chatter of the crowd and the rumble of traffic sound distorted, ominous. My footsteps echo around in front—behind—beside me. Just keep walking in time to the blood in my ears.

"I want to see you bleeding," a woman tells me, stopping in front of me.

"Huh?" I say, looking up, and obviously something about my general demeanor scares the shit out of her, because she suddenly becomes very pale and she stutters out again. . .

"I think you're bleeding."

. . . signaling by pointing to her upper lip and breaking eye contact, walking around me and away quickly. I touch my lip.

Red.

Fuck.

I cut myself shaving this morning, must have opened it up again. I wipe it with the back of my hand, smearing the blood around my upper lip, and carry on—half-running—to the station.

And the train pulls out with the agonized roar of a thousand children wailing in unison. My heart is slowing down somewhat. I can feel the heroin more now. Misjudged the shot, maybe. Too much coke. For once that old fucker Imtiaz was not lying about the quality of his guy's crack.

And on the train a crazy black guy sat singing a kind of spiritual in time with the train's *clack-clacks.*

Because I give it up to Jee-sus!

And people were looking round at one another, smirking, slightly embarrassed by this public display of both insanity and religion—two very taboo subjects in modern British society. He carried on in his West London–Jamaican patois:

Yes I give up to tha Lord!

Because he is the wan Lor'

Tha wan an on-ly Lor'

And I could feel my heart rattling in my rib cage and I started to wonder what would happen if I died right now, if my heart finally gave out, if Vanessa got the call that I was found dead on an underground train with my bloodstream full of cocaine and heroin and I cursed myself silently for being a weak fucking idiot.

Who you gwan call when the judg-ment come?

I say who you gwan call when the judgment come?

When Gabri-el's trumpet sound?

———

Stepping off the train and into the noise and chaos of Euston. Cutting down endless corridors, looking for a way out. Every suitcase a potential bomb. Potential mass slaughter. What kind of world was this? For any of us?

And down down down the escalator.

"Oi! You! Come back!"

But I'm already away—down, down, down—no looking back, not even a glimpse of the devils on my heels, and I don't think I'm ever gonna surface.

36

ADULTHOOD

We argued all night. And the worst thing was that I was arguing from an untenable position. Vanessa was crying hysterically because I had lied to her, because I couldn't even admit that I was high when I walked into the house. The argument had started as soon as I came in and she saw my pupils, as small as pin pricks, and heard my lies muffled through a mouthful of cotton as I tried to tell her that I had only smoked weed and taken some Valium. She asked me if I thought that she was some kind of naïve idiot, and I told her no. But that's what I was treating her like. A naïve idiot.

The argument carried on all night, and at eleven o'clock we were both in bed, bunched up in our separate miseries, her sobbing and red-eyed on one side of the bed, and me alternating between 'tears and anger directed at her but really all about myself and my own weaknesses. I punched the wall and the skin on my knuckle split painfully. And then she said to me: "I am going to leave! I'm going back to New York! I will not have a junkie raise my daughter! If I can't trust you now, how can I trust you with the life of my child? You'll never see her! You'll have nothing to do with her, I swear it!"

And her words finally bludgeon the fact home that this misery that I have been enduring for the past few months is not the end, but the beginning of once again being alive, and I am amazed at how ungrateful I am, and how completely at the mercy of the most base and ignorant part of myself that I am. I realize that I am on the brink of losing everything and being back where I started. Somehow, through dumb luck or divine intervention, I fell in love, truly fell in love for the first time in my rotten, fucked-up life, and I fell in love when I was at my lowest ebb, my worst point, my most destroyed, destitute and bankrupted, and yet somehow this woman saw past all of that and let me into her life, and allowed me an opportunity to reclaim enough of myself that I could have something substantial to offer her and yet, despite having gotten past the worst of it, having done the things that even six months ago would have seemed utterly impossible—detoxing, finding a reason to carry on, seeing the world for the widescreen, Technicolor spectacle it truly can be instead of a black-and-white junk-eye view from underneath a mountain of shit and garbage— I am still a prisoner to the screaming, whining, dying part of my brain that is content to wallow in the gutter for all eternity.

And I know what I have to do.

I have known all along.

I need to see this through to the end, or live forever consumed by the thoughts of what might have been, of what life may have had to offer me, of where those alternate paths might have led.

And I know now, I need to grow up.

37

A GHOST

Vanessa and I were riding the subway, on our way back from the hospital. She had a real pregnant belly now. Our daughter, for we have discovered that it is a little girl, was due to be born in two months. Slowly, my sanity had started to return. Seeing that living thing moving around inside of Vanessa's belly filled me with a giddy joy that three months ago I would have thought was impossible.

The first thing that happened was that I started sleeping through the night. For months I would fall asleep and then find myself wide awake at four in the morning, with nothing to think of but how much I wanted heroin. No matter what I tried, the sleep wouldn't come. When that stopped, and I was able to sleep again, my mind began to heal almost immediately.

———

Still, everything reminded me of junk. Sometimes, walking around the London streets, I would catch the scent of just cooked heroin on the breeze, and it made my stomach churn. Sometimes I dreamed vividly of shooting up, and when I jolted awake my breath was shallow and my heart pounded in my chest. But the days did not seem so impossible anymore. Every day it was getting easier to make the decision to not get high.

We were on the train heading into the West End when they got on. There was a little old lady walking with a cane and a cadaverous-looking man supporting her. I watched them, lulled half asleep by the motion of the train, when my blood suddenly turned to ice as I realized who they were. They recognized me too. Susan tottered over to us, with Jimmy the Scottish junkie from the needle exchange in tow. They sat down opposite us.

"Long time no see," she said.

"All right?" Jimmy grinned.

Vanessa did not know either of them. Until this point, she had never seen Susan's face. I could tell that she sensed that they were people I knew from the heroin scene, because she placed a protective hand over mine. She knew that relapses are made of smaller things than meeting up with old dope buddies.

———

"Hi, Susan," I said eventually. "How have you been?"

"Well . . . not so good. Not so good at all."

They stayed on for a couple of stops. The conversation was vague and circular. She told me that she and Jimmy were living together, and they had found a good doctor near his place in Brixton. I asked her about the cane and she mumbled something about a fucked-up shot of Dexedrine. She was very high: her mouth was slack, and her face looked worn down. A few times she zoned out mid-sentence and her eyes turned up a little in her head. Jimmy was slightly more together.
"I have a job now," she told me, coming back to the conversation.

"That's great."

"I work at the needle exchange. They found funding to take me on as a full-time employee."

"Cool. That's great news."

Susan looked over at Vanessa. Vanessa smiled at her awkwardly.

"You're having a baby," she said.

"Yes. A little girl."

"Congratulations."

———

I could bear this no more, so I squeezed Vanessa's hand and told Susan, "This is our stop." We stood to get off the train. It wasn't our stop, but I felt like I could not breathe properly anymore. Jimmy shook my hand again, and Susan said, "Nice to meet you" as Vanessa waved at her, and we walked out of the train onto the platform.

We stood there together, as the train pulled off into the night. It was a misty, winter evening. We waited in silence for another train.

"Jesus Christ," Vanessa asked eventually, "that was your ex? That was Susan?"

"Yeah."

"Jesus Christ," she said again.

"I know."

I looked over at Vanessa. She was truly beautiful. I don't know what I did to deserve her. I placed a hand over her belly again, and we stood closer, huddling for warmth.

"Isn't life strange?" I whispered to her, as another train pulled into the platform.

38

PEACE

Summer is dying and London is changing again, the colors of the city are darkening and a somber kind of autumnal feeling is on the streets: the skies are fading to magenta in the early evening and the air carries a crisp, sweet chill in it. The gutters are becoming choked with leaves, and every day the child that grows within Vanessa becomes stronger and more alive. Sometimes when we lay in bed together I place my mouth near the smooth roundness of her belly and I have whispered conversations with my child, or I play gentle music like the Cocteau Twins, My Bloody Valentine, or Nick Drake, resting a hand there gently to get a sense of her movements.

It is not just London that is changing, and it is not just the child in Vanessa's belly that is growing. It is happening to me also. At first the process was painful, almost unbearably painful, but now that I have become accustomed to these changes they are a constant source of wonder to me. My body and my mind are experiencing sensations that had been absent for so long that they had become alien to me.

One day I suppose I will have a perspective of these weeks and months that will be radically different from what I am experiencing now. But for now life is almost unbearably vivid. The colors seem too bright at times, the longing that I feel too intense, the love and devotion that I am capable of terrifying in its implication. I am stumbling through the days like a child, wide-eyed and open, lost in the wonderment of all that surrounds me.

EPILOGUE

Brief Encounter

Vanessa was admitted to Homerton Hospital at three o'clock this morning. It seems that the little girl she has been carrying about in her belly is ready to make her appearance. We have decided to wait to name her until we see her face. We picked out all kinds of names but decided that it was unfair to choose before she has even had a chance to draw breath in the outside world. She will tell us her name.

There is a certain irony in the fact that my daughter will be born in the same hospital where I once received my methadone. Vanessa and I have talked and talked and we have come to the decision that it would be best for us to leave London. I hope that London will not become poisoned to me, as Los Angles became. We are considering a move to New York, once our daughter is a little

older. But for now, for certain, we have to leave
London. It just feels like the right thing to do.
Earlier I picked up some things for Vanessa in the
city, before getting back on the train and heading
to the hospital.

RJ boarded the train at Kings Cross, his phan-
tomlike presence filling the carriage with old
memories, tastes, smells: standing in his kitchen
in Hammersmith while he weighed out the
junk in the bathroom and his daughter absently
watched cartoons in the next room and talked to
friends on the phone . . . *"Darren? He's a fuckin'
arsehole . . . I ain't fuckin' desperate, you know?"* . . .
and having to split from his flat with the gear and
find somewhere else to fix, despite the sweat running off me in torrents and the puke and the shit
all about to vacate my body violently, because his
family thinks he is off the gear and dealing weed
instead.

"Jesus, RJ, how are you?" I ask him. He jumps and
turns—his placid old junky's face has filled out a
little in the intervening year.

"What the fuck? Fuckin' hell long time no see,
mate. . . . What the fuck happened to you?"

"Ah you know, I kicked a little while back, and
then . . ." I raise my palms and shrug.

"You off now?"

I laugh a little. "Yeah. For the time being. You still
dealing?"

"Nah . . . I'm off the gear right now, too. Coming up to six months. Just got out a meeting at the Cross."

"How is it?"

"Shit. But what are you gonna do?"

RJ has been in the game for a long time. When I first met him he was already fucked up. A ghost. An earthbound phantom. His patient junkie walk. His arms, white and thin, veins long since retreated under mounds of old hardened scar tissue. He told me he used to have to soak them in scalding water for twenty minutes before he could even attempt to hit a vein.

"How's your brother doing?"

RJ's face darkened. He made a motion with his hands and took a sharp inhalation of breath, which suggested that Mike had started using crack. "The coke bugs got 'im," he said quietly, "ate the flesh off him. He died screaming."

And in a scream of gray metal, tinny voices chattering from the PA system and echoing through black tunnels, RJ is vanished again, lost to God, and I think, He'll be back. They always come back. And it's true. The only cure is death. I am convinced of that. But everyone is sick in one way or another, and the only cure for that is death, also. "Life can be considered a terminal illness." Who said that? Well fuck . . . what does it matter?

———

Everybody is fading out. The signal is getting weak. Sometimes people vanish in front of my eyes as if they had never been there. Then in a burst of static they are back. I am eating pills every morning to keep the ghosts away. When things start to get too clear, too focused, it hurts my head.

There is business to take care of now. There are lives that depend on me, as terrifying and strange as that concept might be. The birth of my daughter is rattling to the foundations my long-held assumption that everybody is essentially alone in this world.

The train keeps moving.
I keep moving too.
Destination, anywhere.
Amen.

New York
January 2007

ACKNOWLEDGMENTS

This book would never have been written without the following people being in my life:

Vanessa O'Neill, my wife and muse, who I'm glad to say doesn't mind me airing our dirty laundry in public. Thank you for giving me a second shot at life.

My daughter, Nico Estrella O'Neill, who gives me a reason to keep going every single day.

My parents, Rose and Frank, who will never read this book (not because they don't know, but because they DO know). You bailed my ass out of trouble more times than I can ever recall, and what do I do in return? I write a book. I know, and I'm sorry.

These people helped ease this book into the world:

My agent, Michael Murphy, at the Max Literary Agency and Social Club, who believes in my writing as much as I do (and that's a lot because I'm an egomaniac), and worked his ass off to get my stuff into print. I can never repay you, but I can thank you . . .

The team at Harper Perennial, who obviously have wonderful taste in authors, and who have done an amazing job with this book. You really made me feel like I am a part of the family. Extra-special thanks to Carrie Kania, Michael Signorelli, and Amy Baker for all of their hard work.

These people kept me alive:

Clean Needles Now, the Methadone Alliance, Jerry Schoenkopf at the Telesis Foundation, all the other fuck-ups in Cri-Help circa summer of 2000, Genesis House, the National Drug Users Network, and the Marylebone Practice.

These people first published me:

Contemporary Press, Erin O'Mara at *Black Poppy* magazine, *3am* magazine, *Dogmatika*, Laura Hird, and *Savage Kick* magazine.

Just Say No to the War on Drugs.

About the author

About the book

Read on

Insights,
Interviews
& More...

Meet Tony O'Neill

Ferny Chung

TONY O'NEILL is the author of several books, including *Digging the Vein*, *Seizure Wet Dreams*, and *Songs from the Shooting Gallery*. His essays, poems, and short stories have appeared extensively online and in print, and he has been described by *The Guardian* as "a man who has taken the term 'rock-and-roll poet' to its furthest edges." He is a survivor of heroin, crack, rehab, fatherhood, a stint in the Brian Jonestown Massacre, Kenickie, and a tour with Marc Almond's band. He lives in New York with his wife and daughter. ∾

In Conversation with Sebastian Horsley

I met the artist, dandy, and writer Sebastian Horsley when I first returned from Los Angeles to London. I had shown up to a Narcotics Anonymous meeting in Soho with the intention of scoring drugs. My logic was this: If you want drugs, you have to go to where the drug addicts are.

I didn't score drugs that day, but I did meet Sebastian. He was dressed in a powder-pink suit, and looked as unhappy as I was to be in a twelve-step meeting. When it was his turn to speak, Sebastian held the floor for quite a while to complain about how dull his days were now that he wasn't smoking crack. He also talked about some mysterious art project he was about to embark on. A few months later, I saw Sebastian again. He was in the newspaper, having gone to the Philippines and having had himself literally crucified for the sake of art.

Sebastian wrote a wonderful memoir, Dandy in the Underworld *(Harper Perennial), and I wrote a magazine article on him that lead to a busy correspondence and friendship. A meeting in the United States was thwarted when customs denied his visa on the grounds of "moral turpitude." So, instead of conducting the following conversation over a few glasses of absinthe in a dark bar, it was done via the much less glamorous medium of the computer . . .*

Sebastian Horsley: *You were a rock star and now you are a writer. Why the fuck do you want to write books when you can write songs you daft cunt? Surely you know all art is failed music?*

Tony O'Neill: Well the tortuous thing about being in a band is the necessity of having other people around you. Having four or five strong and distinct personalities all involved in the creative process is usually a disaster. You start off trying to make filet mignon and end up with a packet of instant soup, because no fucker can make up their mind. That's ▶

3

In Conversation with Sebastian Horsley
(continued)

why for every Ramones, there are two dozen
Coldplays. The moment I knew I could no
longer stand to be in the music industry was
probably when I realized I had been standing
in a decrepit rehearsal room in northern
London for two weeks arguing with a
drummer about what kind of bass drum
pattern he was going to play in the chorus
of a song. I knew there was no joy in what
I was doing any more.

I was eighteen when I played for Marc
Almond and Kenickie, the two bands I was
involved in that drew audiences, commanded
media attention, all of that stuff. Fast forward
seven years or so, I'm playing in a club in
Brighton with four people in the audience
(if you include the guide dog that the blind
guy had brought with him), sipping from
a bottle of methadone in between songs to
keep me going. I was either done with music,
or music was done with me. Either way the
end result was the same.

When I started writing books, I applied
all of the lessons that I learned writing songs:
Keep it moving. If in doubt, cut it out. In and
out in three minutes or less. Don't let 'em get
bored. *Bam, bam, bam*—verse, chorus middle
eight. And I didn't have four other people
standing over my shoulder arguing with
me about the best way to write a sentence.

S.H.: *What are you most ashamed of?*

T.O.: I don't feel shame. I know that if I found
out I was dying tomorrow my only real regret
would be I didn't do more of everything.
I survived a life-and-death struggle with
myself, minus a few teeth and a lot of veins.
Apart from that everything still works okay.
The only times I really feel regret is when I feel
that—or whatever reason—I have behaved
too nicely in a social situation. The one and
only time I appeared on *Top of the Pops* [for
my American readers, *TOTP* was the biggest
music-related TV show in England] I just
stood there and played music. Looking back,
I should have vomited or pissed on somebody

while we were on-air. I was assuming I'd be on there again. I was saving myself.

S.H.: *To justify ones existence writing has to be extraordinary. If it's ordinary, it's less than worthless; it's clutter. There are more writers now than readers, which suits the world, as everyone is talking and nobody is listening. Those who have lived can't write, while those who can write haven't lived. The chief knowledge a man gets from reading books is the knowledge that very few of them are worth reading. Waffle, waffle, waffle. Look, why should anyone read your fucking book?*

T.O.: Finding a good book is like finding a needle in a haystack. When it's a really, really good book, it's like finding a needle full of strong Chinese heroin in a haystack. Look, I'm a reader too. I know there's a lot of terrible writing out there. Writers complain that the review sections of newspapers are getting smaller, that people would rather watch reality TV than read books, that text messaging is killing literature, all of that stuff. Three words: WRITE. BETTER. BOOKS. Writers have to compete. They have to up their game. Most of the big writers out there, the ones who command attention in the Booker Prize lists, the "Best of" lists in major newspapers, the critics' darlings—I mean, it's fucking sewerage. The books they produce are garbage! Intellectual masturbation. If I want to see someone jerk off, I'll go to a peep show and pay 25 cents, not twenty-five dollars for a hardcover book. Now, this Q&A is for the back of the book. So I'm assuming that either someone has already bought the book in which case it's too late. You're stuck with me! Or they're standing in a bookstore, flipping through it. So to answer your question: "Why should anyone read *my* fucking book?"—flip back to the first chapter. Read the first chapter. It won't take long. Go on!

Okay, you're done? Now you know where I'm at, the kind of writing I do, and what ▶

In Conversation with Sebastian Horsley
(*continued*)

you're going to get when you hand over your money. If you're already disgusted, then there are a lot of books by the "other" writers all over this shop. Go ahead. You deserve each other.

S.H.: *Can evil be a spiritual experience too? Tell me when it has been for you.*

T.O.: It would depend on what your definition of *evil* is. I consider myself a pretty moral person. I do recognize that my sense of morality is probably at odds with what most people consider "moral" behavior. When the laws are unjust or archaic—in my opinion—it is your duty to disobey them. As a substitute for so-called authentic spiritual experiences, shooting a speedball comes pretty close. With all of the talk of "spiritual awakenings" in NA, I never experienced anything approximating what I got by injecting a combination of heroin and cocaine into my veins. I am aware someone somewhere might consider that act to be evil. If that's the case, then, yes, that act of evil felt pretty fucking good.

S.H.: *Would you rather have written* Tintin *or the collective works of Brecht?*

T.O.: I've never read any *Tintin*. But I do know that had I written *Tintin* I'd be much wealthier than if I'd written the collected works of Brecht. So I'll take *Tintin*. I would love to write something that has the kind of mass-appeal that the Bible or Harry Potter has. Why not? Intellectual snobbery is only something you can really afford if you're rich.

S.H: *Reading* Mein Kampf *does not make a Fascist. Reading the Bible does not make a Christian. Reading* Das Kapital *does not make a Marxist. Does reading* Down and Out on Murder Mile *make a junkie? Discuss.*

T.O.: Anybody seriously interested in Christianity will read the Bible at some point.

An aspiring Fascist would probably have to knuckle down and read *Mein Kampf*. Someone studying Marxism will have to pick up *Das Kapital*. The difference is that a junkie rarely makes the decision to become a junkie because of some intellectual position. Believe me, I had been shooting dope for a long time before I would even admit to myself that I was an addict.

Heroin—all drugs, really—don't need cheerleaders. People will try them. Some people will like them enough to keep doing them. Others won't. I didn't become a heroin addict because I enjoyed the books of William S. Burroughs or Herbert Huncke. I became a heroin addict because I liked heroin. A lot.

I never wrote *Down and Out* as an advertisement or an enticement to do anything. I'd say the book probably hammers home something few other books talk about that addiction does: Addiction, in the long term, is a pretty fucking boring business. It's routine. Even shooting up becomes mundane if you do it long enough. For me, today, waking up and not wanting to be dead is a pretty novel experience. If I had to sum this book up in one word, it would be *optimism*. It's an optimistic book. After all, as Samuel Beckett said: "When you're up to your neck in shit, there's nothing you can do but sing." ∾

On Writing *Down and Out on Murder Mile*

by Tony O'Neill

DIGGING THE VEIN, my first novel, left out a huge chunk of the "real" story of my period of addiction. I suppose this was because at the time of writing it, a lot of the issues were still unresolved. The two main threads that I felt I needed to explore more were my second marriage (which I didn't mention at all in *Digging*), and the years in London. My London period was dispensed with in one chapter in the first book, when in fact in was as complex and involved a story as the years in Los Angeles were.

The second marriage was difficult to write about because I didn't have any distance from it then. It took me a few years to be able to start picking through that and writing about it in a way that made sense to me. Every time I sit down to write I do not sit down to write memoir, I don't feel bound by the facts. I see the facts as just building blocks that I can make a story out of. In fact, some of my most personal writing is the stuff that I don't readily identify as being about my past. That way I can reveal stuff in oblique ways, and get away with it.

London was still all around me when writing *Digging,* and it took me to be away from London to actually re-create a version of that city in my mind's eye. Just as it took me a while out of the methadone clinics to be able to process that period enough to try to re-create it.

Talking of novels that inspired *Down and Out*, I suppose I look toward people who had the same outlook on the autobiographical novel as I do: one of my favorite books about addiction is Alexander Trocchi's *Cain's Book*. Another is William S. Burroughs's *Junky*. When one looks at the biography of both writers and the facts that were presented in the books, you can see that they were both very selective on what they revealed. I think the tabloid age of everybody having to know everything, and the American addiction to ▶

confessing all, of opening up your guts to anyone willing to pay to gawp at them is pretty sickening, truth be told. I never wanted to stand up and "share" in recovery meetings, and I don't use my writing as a chance to do that either.

Herbert Huncke was and is a huge influence on me. *The Herbert Huncke Reader* is one of the most important and influential books I have ever read. I love his mix of high art, and barroom-type conversational storytelling. To me he represents the soul of the Beat canon, but he is sadly one of the least read of the Beats.

A modern example of a writer who treads this line very well is Dan Fante, whose Bruno Dante trilogy were a big inspiration to me. Just seeing someone else mining a roughly similar vein to me—and getting published—was very impactful.

My writing space at the moment is much better than it used to be. I have a desk now, and a little office too. It's an old wooden desk my wife and I found in a used furniture store—it's big, heavy, and has a few scrapes and scratches. It's perfect. I do a lot of my writing in notebooks, the ninety-nine-cent composition books you buy in drug stores. I'm pretty fractured in how I write, I guess. I keep random things: I have napkins in some of my boxes with first drafts of chapters from my book jotted down on them, for instance. I wrote 90 percent of *Seizure Wet Dreams* (a collection of poems), on my mother-in-law's computer because I didn't have one when we first moved to New York City.

Down and Out on Murder Mile came together in my usual, fragmented way. Writing books for me is kind of like absentmindedly picking at scabs. I mean, I didn't even realize I was writing this book until I had three-fourths of it finished. Undoubtedly, out of anything I have written so far, *Down and Out* is easily my favorite. ❧

The *Down and Out on Murder Mile* Soundtrack Album

MUSIC IS VERY, VERY IMPORTANT to how I write. I have as many musical influences as I have literary influences. Sometimes an odd lyrical turn of phrase in a song can inspire a story or prompt a memory that produces something new.

I was a musician for most of my life, so I think of writing in musical terms. I think that a novel should have the immediacy and the propulsion of a good song. I often listen to music as I write, and the choice of music can dictate the tone and direction of what I write. With that in mind, here is a soundtrack album for *Down and Out on Murder Mile*: a collection of songs that were playing when the action unfolded, or songs that sum up the mood of the story. . . . Turn it up loud and enjoy . . .

Primal Scream's "Autobahn 66" (*Evil Heat*)

Primal Scream became the unofficial band of that summer. Vanessa and I must have seen them play half a dozen times, at least. This pulsing, hypnotic track was rarely off our stereo.

The Brian Jonestown Massacre's "Evergreen" (*Methadrone*)

Recorded way before my involvement with the band. A beautiful, heavy song. At a rehearsal, Anton once shot me up with dope and blew out one of my best veins. I can never forgive him. But it doesn't make this song any less perfect.

The Ramones's "Beat on the Brat" (*The Ramones*)

This is possibly the best rock song about physically abusing a child ever written. It makes me think of good times. London, the Queens Golden Jubilee. Lots of strong

MDMA, booze, and the sense that I could breathe for the first time in years.

The Gun Club's "Yellow Eyes" (*Mother Juno*)

I first heard this song on a busted cassette player, while someone drove me to an NA meeting. I was half dead, the first time I had ever experienced three days without heroin. I still get chills when I listen to Jeffrey Lee Pierce's fractured blues howl.

My Bloody Valentine's "When You Sleep" (*Loveless*)

This album was playing when Vanessa and I met. We fell in love to this album, and this song became one of my favorites. For me it's the greatest rock album of all time. A staggering achievement, and relentlessly beautiful as well.

Kenickie's "Come Out 2nite" (*At the Club*)

This is my favorite Kenickie song. There is a melancholy at the heart of Kenickie that I think a lot of people miss. It's hard for me to listen to Kenickie sometimes. It fills me with many memories, some wonderful. Sometimes I get sad hearing this stuff. At the time, I didn't know what kind of hell was in store for me after I'd leave the band. Those days were the last innocent times I had.

The Fall's "Bingo-Master's Break-Out!" (*Live at the Witch Trials*)

I hated being in northern England as a kid. The Fall were one of the first bands that made me feel a little like I belonged up there. I hated Oasis, all of that tracksuits, lager, and bowl haircuts bullshit. The Fall were one of the few bands from the north that weren't afraid to be intelligent.

The White Sport's "Scag Lover" (single)

My favorite song about doing drugs. It's messy, silly, and there's something ▶

The *Down and Out on Murder Mile* Soundtrack Album *(continued)*

hypnotic about hearing someone repeatedly imploring you to shoot some heroin over a pulsing homemade dance beat. I listened to it a lot at the time, and, yeah, I shot dope listening to it.

Soft Cell's "Say Hello, Wave Goodbye" (*Non-Stop Erotic Cabaret*)

One of my best memories is playing this song acoustically with Marc Almond at a show in Southport. Marc was responsible for a huge part of my musical education. I came to him as something of a clean slate, willing and wanting to learn. I remember him pressing a bunch of vinyl by Johnny Thunders, Wire, Jayne Country, and Nick Cave into my hands, and telling me to listen. Thank you, Marc.

Lou Reed's "Sad Song" (*Berlin*)

This one puts me back in LA, at the worst of it. I can smell freshly cooked Mexican heroin when I hear this song. It's so beautiful, and so heartbreaking. I would love to write something as lovely as this song one day.

David Bowie's "New Career in a New Town" (*Low*)

I love all of Bowie's seventies albums, but *Low* is my favorite. Yes, I have chosen an instrumental song. It's the only one of his instrumentals I love as much as his vocal tracks. If this book were a movie, this is the song that would come on as the credits rolled. ❧

Three Poems

by Tony O'Neill

hey, Randal

hey, Randal
i was thinking about you today
remembering you in the bathroom of
   Goldfingers
and you were saying
don't marry her!
you're fucking crazy!
i lived with her for two years
she's fucking nuts, man
then you offered me a line of crystal meth
and i ignored your advice

well you were right
she was fucking nuts and the marriage
   didn't last
and the drummer from the band we saw
went on to marry Lisa Marie Presley
that didn't last either
i guess everyone got fucked over that night

hey, Randal
remember when we stayed up for 3 nights
getting high
and we ended up in The Spotlight
and everything seemed out of focus
6 in the morning and we were
snorting speed off the bar with a leather fag
   called Marty

i went to take a piss
became scared by my reflection
watched two old guys blowing each other
right out in the open
and then we were off on your bike
roaring down Hollywood Boulevard
pulling up alongside an LAPD prowl car
and you smiled and waved at them
before the light changed and we roared away
weaving in and out of traffic
steered by the hand of God?

hey, Randal
remember out on that balcony
after we'd bailed our coke dealer out ▶

Three Poems *(continued)*

and waited for him outside of the station
so we could pick up two eight balls
and he said
you white boys are fucking crazy
grinning a big wide grin

and full of cocaine and speed
and pills and booze
i said you were my brother and that i
    loved you
then i got embarrassed
but you said
it's OK, i know
we're the same you and me
just don't ever forget this

and then, Randal
hell found us
and the party ground to a halt

Maus showed me pictures of you
in the period we lost touch
you looked older, bigger
haunted
you'd grown a crazy Anton LaVey moustache
and sat around the house for a year
smoking crack
and checking the door was still locked

and me?
that's an old story
another ex-wife
two stints in rehab
a tattoo I don't remember getting
and some missing teeth
(you can fill in the gaps, my friend)

but hey, Randal
i saw the picture in Cambodia
when Maus rented your apartment and sold
    your car
and sent you over there to get better
with our friend Dave

you looked thinner healthier
that crazy moustache was gone
the haunted look was gone
and the pain was gone

you looked like my brother again
and the picture they used at your memorial
    service
is the one that really stuck in my head

an abandoned truck
thrown from the bike
neck snapped neatly
with some new girl
and Dave B at your side
you died as you lived
at full throttle

hey, Randal
you really got it made
in death you are perfect
ageless
reckless and beautiful
forever

1319 iris circle #3

another final point had been reached:
another grief-silent 3 a.m.
she placed the gun under her chin
heavy with Xanax and heroin
and told me that this time, she fucking
    meant it

I screamed at her not to be so stupid
and to put the gun down for christ's sake
she looked at me with her pinned
    shell-shocked eyes
and conceded

the things I had seen with this woman —
needles probing breasts for shrinking,
    retreating veins
cocaine induced grand mal seizures
and armies of cock swallowed for a balloon
    of dope or a
rock

she handed me her father's handgun with a
    resigned sob
and I placed it back under the bookshelf

I smile sadly, in light of what came next
to think that I told her ▶

Three Poems *(continued)*

If you can just hang on, things are bound
    to improve

she made me a liar, too —
the woman who dug the hole
I've been trying to write myself out of
ever since

23-10-03

all of the years
surviving myself,
american and ex-wives
do not make me worthy

of one second
of your laughter

you smile
and my universe wrenches open
setting me adrift
in a world as alien and vast
as the deepest most desolate ocean

the sight of your languid
miniature, light brown legs
stretching—twisting over one another
lost in imaginary worlds
fills my chest with something
so sweetpainful, tangibly real
that the words are torn from my throat

I think of all of the alternate paths,
choices and intrusions of fate
that could have led me
somewhere, anywhere but here

and I am forced
to doubt
my previous conclusions
on the existence
of higher powers ∾

These poems originally appeared in
Seizure Wet Dreams *by Tony O'Neill,*
Social Disease, London, 2006